Pavel Hak was born in Czecl
France in 1986, he studied ph
novelist and playwright, he w
second novel, is his first book
In his own words, he 'investigates contemporary violence, mechanisms of domination and the moral and physical torture inflicted on individuals'. He lives in Paris.

Sniper

Pavel Hak

Translated by Gerry Feehily

A complete record for this book can be obtained
from the British Library on request

First published in French as *Sniper* by
Éditions Tristram, France

First published in English in 2005 by Serpent's Tail,
4 Blackstock Mews, London N4 2BT
website: www.serpentstail.com

Designed and typeset at Neuadd Bwll, Llanwrtyd Wells

Printed by Legoprint Spa, Italy

With the support of the
Culture 2000 programme
of the European Union

Education and Culture

Culture 2000

The author and the editors at Éditions Tristram thank agnès b. for her support on publication of the French edition

1

My duty is to kill. To deal a lethal blow (in a split second) to whoever is condemned to die. By whom? Why? War doesn't allow for questions. Dissidents, fleeing men and women, enemy soldiers, rebels financed by foreign powers, children, the old, nothing but words to describe a single and self-same reality: my target! To deal a lethal blow. To kill. Time, which suffocates us, and death, which pursues us, are both invisible. Can we stop time and overcome death by killing soldiers, peasants, mercenaries, intruders coming from who knows what part of the world? To destroy. Annihilate. I will let no one leave here alive. All it takes is one survivor and the irreparable happens: accusation. And with that dirty bitch comes verdict and sentence. Because the moment a mouth opens, a black hole comes into the world and with it a moment of suspense: what will this mouth say? What truth is it going to spew out? People are greedy for news. Groans and whimpers speak volumes. Damn! The human mouth has an annoying habit of talking, a defect we just don't need any more. Accursed race, I'll turn you into a heap of minced meat! Worshippers of the verb, would-be spewers of blasphemous speech, malicious orators, all you stinking hyenas, your brains are about to be blown to bits! Complaints, demands, peace proposals, proclamations of new laws, impassioned speeches as to how things are, there's no place for you: you've got to be eliminated one by one, systematically, in order of appearance. Shall I take an oath on that? When I'm finished, there won't be a single babbling mouth left. Once I've fired the last shot, order will reign. I take part in this conflict to wipe out that foul pedlar of insane chatter that is man. My gun's duty is to stop up that vile source of words which exists only to besmirch, stir up revolt and encourage disobedience. If only they didn't talk, if only they didn't pour forth crazy speeches about their right to life, to happiness and land (which they say belongs to them, when it's always been ours), there wouldn't be any more war. There's a war on because of too many babbling mouths. Too many slanders. He who accepts order and abides by the law can never be the cause of evil. Source of misfortune. The reason why it takes guns to settle disputes.

2

As dawn approaches, roofs and then white chalk walls emerge from the dark. A light mist obscures stables, barns and farm machines standing beside vegetable patches covered in hoar frost. Shortly after the cock's insistent crow and then some bellowing here and there from beasts chilled to the bone, the mist, dispersed by a breeze, begins to lift. The vales, silver in the heights, blue at the bottom of the gorge, come more into focus. The dawn (first nothing but a diffuse light) rises from behind the mountain crests. A dazzling yellow glow heralds the break of day when a mortar shell, followed by ten more, explodes in the village square. The missiles, fired with great precision, hit houses, destroying roofs, woodwork, walls; a shell explodes a few yards from the church, blowing out its stained-glass windows and setting off the bell in its tower. Other buildings are hit. And while flames shoot out of gutted roofs, villagers with coats hastily thrown on, eyes wide with fear, rush from their houses, several of which have thick smoke gushing out. Not a single villager, nor a single animal locked up in its byre, can withstand the panic the explosions have triggered. Bewildered men and animals look all around. Hardly has the whistling of approaching mortar ceased than the rumble of military vehicles fills the air. The roar of motors, the clanking of tank tracks, a commander yelling orders and shots fired into the air proclaim that the army has arrived: a convoy of armoured cars appears on the road leading to the village, seals it off and invades the main square. The villagers, assault weapons pointed at them, freeze in their doorways. Armoured cars throb, officers watch their troops as, after jumping down from army trucks, they level their automatic rifles at people's chests. 'Don't move!' Having grasped, the minute the first mortar fell, what is about to happen, a young man comes out of his house with a hunting rifle; before he can even raise his weapon, a dozen automatic rifles erupt and he collapses, his throat torn open. The commander barks orders. The people who lived in the same house as the young man are rounded up, beaten, insulted, handcuffed: the soldiers herd them with rifle butts to the church wall, wrench open their coats, bare their chests. The villagers, forced by the soldiers to listen as the commander yells, condemning these traitors for disobedience and complicity in the thwarted attack, tremble at the sight of the assassinated young man's family. The quickly assembled firing squad loads rifles. 'Fire!' screams the commander. The bodies are still twitching on the ground as the soldiers push the villagers towards buses lined up by the burned-out houses. In the midst of the screaming women and crying children, an old peasant, covered in a blanket spattered with lumps of bloody flesh, rushes out of the ruins of his farm: 'My herd, my cows!' An officer grabs the old man by the throat. 'Stop yelling, old man! When mortars start falling, it's time to kneel and pray!' 'My animals, blown to pieces,' the old man moans, wiping gobs of runny minced meat off his forehead. The officer shakes the old man, aims his gun at a horse running amok in the street. 'Obsessed with the carcasses of your animals? Don't worry, they can't feel anything.' And he shoots the panic-stricken animal dead. Then, pointing at a young girl huddled between her mother and an old woman, he says: 'That your niece?' The old man nods. The officer pushes the women aside, grabs the young girl, contemplates her eyes, her barely budding breasts, then takes her by the back of the neck. 'Show me your room.' The young girl, half dead from fear, stammers, 'I don't have my own room.' Before he pushes her with muscular arms towards the house, he whispers an order that has the soldiers doubled up with laughter. 'Round up all the decent-looking ones and line them up in the barn. But move it, you've only got half an hour!' While the soldiers hunt for women (and loot whatever houses haven't been hit by mortar fire) some of the villagers manage to escape. They scramble through the mud, steer clear of leaping flames, hide behind clouds of smoke, slip past the lookouts, find a country road, leave behind them that maze of gutted houses standing on scorched earth, climb up a slope, walk along a river, slip and slide in the wet grass, disappear into the forest. Back in the village square, the commander (leaving the house on his own) yells the evacuation order. And while the soldiers push the last of the villagers on to a bus, a trailer full of corpses, loaded far from prying eyes in the shadows of the barn, makes its way to a trench dug in a field behind the stables. In every other direction, the soldiers launch incendiary mortars, burning tractors and other farm machines, plant landmines, pull down electric lines, shoot into bushes where – 'You never know!' – fugitives might be hiding. Ready at last, the military convoy makes way first for a lorry carrying food, flour, homemade plum brandy and meat stolen from the cellars of looted houses; then for the buses crammed with villagers. Mission accomplished? The commander issues the order to move out, armoured cars and jeeps trundle past, and a forgotten radio crackles in the dawn of the deserted village (above which some last shreds of morning mist mix with the smoke which rises from the ruins).

3

By the window in overheated HQ, the commander lights a cigarette, then, the muscles in his face contracting, he turns towards the officers standing to attention. 'The intensity of these air raids has slowed down activity in the border zone; our army has had to fall back, our soldiers to dig in, our tanks to stay hidden in underground shelters.' The commander screws his eyes up. 'What do they take us for? Yokels? Simpletons? They increase the number of air raids, they bombard our positions, smash our infrastructure; but we have weapons and means too, wouldn't you agree?' 'Yes, commander!' the officers reply in unison. The commander scrutinises his subordinates. 'If they think that with a few bombs we'll just lie down and roll over...' The officers snigger. The commander crushes the remains of his glowing cigarette with the heel of his boot. 'They organise air raids, we'll organise terror!' The officers, turning pale, fall silent. The commander points at a map taped to the wall. 'Once our artillery has achieved its objective of softening the terrain, our soldiers will move civilians out of their holes, the police will direct refugee convoys, and paramilitary units will take care of reprisals.' The commander looks each officer in the eye. 'What do you think? Murder, rape, summary executions, torture, genocide, crimes against humanity, all these atrocities are part of our strategy. We're going to exploit every aspect of war to the hilt: the weapon of starvation decimates the civilian population, racial hatred sets the countryside aflame, mass expulsions complete ethnic cleansing. But don't forget…' The commander stares at his officers. '… terror must be organised.' The officers nod. 'We're going to create confusion and uncertainty; we'll gain ground in a chaos of doubt. So they say our troops commit war crimes? Then we'll execute twice as many traitors, clamp dissidents in irons and drag them through the streets of the capital, increase police harassment, exacerbate tensions between communities, arrest opposition leaders, hang innocents in public squares, carry out more assassinations! Resistants are holed up in the ruins of conquered cities? We'll flush them out! So they bare their breasts crying freedom? We'll chain them to our tanks. And all the time our propaganda will repeat, relentlessly, over and over, that if we give up our homes and holy places we will be guilty of having forsaken our country!' The commander looks at his officers, notes with satisfaction that their hands are trembling. 'And the women?' He opens the door of overheated HQ, breathes the freezing air in the corridor, yells: 'Guards, bring the bitches in!' A dozen girls wearing dresses with outrageously plunging necklines walk in. The commander orders them to line up against the wall, looks at their carefully selected bodies, then addresses the officers (whose closed faces betray not the slightest emotion). 'The women will be held in cellars, subjected to humiliations and sexual abuse. Torture will teach them to be ashamed of what they are; rape never to speak of what has happened to them! They will suffer the psychological ravages of abuse, will be physically marked, mentally destroyed. Many will become pregnant, others will be contaminated by venereal diseases; every single one of them will live in constant fear, develop suicidal tendencies, suffer from depression and phobias. And if some of them die under torture, too bad: there're enough to go round (some barely twelve years old).' Smiling, the commander walks before his stock-still officers. 'Coshes, knives, impalement, baseball bats, electric shocks, freezing-cold cells, everything will serve our purpose: to smash human rights! And this objective will never be achieved if the women aren't reduced to slavery.' The officers swallow. The commander pulls out his revolver. 'Do you follow me, you pack of scumbags? Our dictatorship will show the whole world that when a state is strong it isn't punished, whatever crimes it commits.' The officers (as one) unzip their flies and grab hold of their rigid cocks.

4

The messenger stops high up on the mountainside; the ravine beneath him, strewn with blocks of granite torn out of the rock face by the torrents that rush down the gullies during the spring thaw, sparkles with a sombre lustre, its slopes covered in a mantle of winter ice. Leaning against a boulder, he digs his heels into a crack in the rock; he looks down to the bottom of the ravine, looks up along the slope on the other side, searching for a trail or path, looks back down the ravine again, follows the river bed, peers at the opening to a mine shaft and spots an old stone bridge half destroyed by the bombs. This is where he must go. Past the bridge, the same landscape stretches away as far as the eye can see: an arid mountain, stone, granite blocks, frozen earth; and a road cut into the mountainside (with sticks of dynamite). The messenger gazes at this gash in the rock; beyond the mountain, over on the other side, lies the industrial valley, its bridges and factories destroyed, its warehouses and oil reservoirs burned. Everything, the streets, administrative buildings, railway lines and public squares, shows signs of having been hit by air raid and mortar shell. To find a way past these collapsed walls, ash heaps, avoiding corpses which (scattered all over the place, like leaflets of absurd propaganda) clutter the footpaths, clog the gutters and lie strewn over patches of waste ground, such will be his task. (The dead, no one collects them any more: the last burial must have taken place a month ago.) Then another task awaits him: to find the house where the man he must speak to lives. Explain to him why he has come, and who has sent him. Winning this man's trust won't be easy – since those who have sent him are asking for the impossible. As the tale is told the man will listen in silence, then lower his gaze to contain the emotion the news has aroused in him, then for a long time he will look at the street, strewn with shrapnel, charred wood beams and broken roof tiles. No one and nothing (excepting the will to live) can help him. The messenger's gaze turns away from the other side of the mountain. The stone bridge (spanning the dry river bed), the road blown out of the granite – this is where he must get to first (avoiding crevasses, walking carefully along the ravine's edge – so many dangerous traps for a man exhausted by a long day's walk). His gaze now falling on a figure on the other side near the summit, he is not surprised. A peasant? Another messenger? Like himself, someone has crossed the mountain with news for the people who have stayed behind in the city, is bringing them food or is coming to receive orders issued in all likelihood from one of the besieged city's air-raid shelters. The peasant walks along the slope with the confident step of one used to steep mountain paths, then stops for breath, leaning against a rock where, practically in the same place, a missile smashed into the granite (yesterday, the day before?). Then the peasant raises his eyes towards the sky (alerted by a whistling noise which, to ears traumatised by war, announces an air raid) when the muffled sound of a gunshot breaks the mountain silence (just as the peasant, having determined that the sky is empty, wonders whether he has the strength to reach the city) and his head explodes. The messenger overcomes an instinctive urge to turn away; but it is vital, before the peasant falls, that he trace the bullet's trajectory and find out where the sniper is firing from. The murderer must be hunkered down in a place where he can survey not only the tundra the peasant has come from (and where the messenger now stands) but also the industrial valley, the city under siege, the road leading to the border, the border checkpoint and the refugee camp (recently built). The bullet having struck him straight in the face, the peasant is knocked off his feet, his arms are flung out, one of his legs looking as though it is taking one more step towards the city, then the power of the bullet's impact throws him off course: the peasant turns (like a spinning top) upon himself, then collapses, his chest covered in gobs of blood and brain, and falls in the dust between rock and clumps of earth. Realising that the man (who has just been killed) has saved his life (for had the man not been killed, he, the messenger, would have taken the same path towards the mountain summit and fallen prey to the sniper in exactly the same place), the messenger quickly works out the bullet's trajectory, looks up towards the mountain top, seeking the killer's hiding place. Not a single clue (a puff of smoke, the glint of a gun barrel, the gunsight reflecting the sky) reveals where the assassin is hunkered down; apart from a gully that has cut a natural trench in the rock, the only possible place is the concrete entrance to an underground gallery, concealed by blocks of recently dynamited granite.

5

I can see everything. Besieged city. Ruins. Sky. Landscape. To see, to be aware of the slightest movement, is my job. Not a single enemy movement (that is, not a single human movement) escapes my attention. My concentration is unflagging. What is a sniper? One who aims true. The desire to kill is a primary urge. Formed in the womb, it flourishes after birth: kill the father! And they condemn me? Why such approbation? You have to construct a mountain of inhibitions to repress the urge to kill. Kill. Kill. Displacing this urge has been the history of mankind. The hunt, war, politics and sport, the stock market, the economy; man's unconscious is peopled with rivals. Masters, adversaries, chiefs, tyrants, competitors, bosses, they are legion. All ripe for the killing! What work it is to direct such an impulse! I load my gun. A woman appears in the doorway of a ruined house, a bucket in her hand. She must go through a gate and cross the street; the only well that hasn't yet been poisoned is in a garden I watch night and day. Are you dying of thirst? I aim. The woman crossing the street falls, her head blown to bits. Prey to doubts? Not I. I shoot. Once man's thoughts get bogged down in doubts, his convictions do too. Without a clear head, how can you aim true at those you wish to kill? Without a lucid outlook, the sniper dies. Fire! There's no other way in the world; it's here, beneath this sky, that you must kill. Despite a flood of pretend worlds of all kinds, this is the only one that matters, the one we give birth to in aiming true. Go on, get your buckets and fetch some water. Come into my sights! The bodies of parched survivors make my struggle real. It is they (their bodies) the sniper seeks out. The only worldview worth considering is that where man and the universe are one (ah, those two lovers – man, the universe – locked in an embrace). But a well-aimed bullet tears them apart. I load my gun again. A group of children, pursued by a panic-stricken female (no doubt their mother), arouses my interest. It's a long time since one of my bullets went clean though a brat's arse! Despite which, it's on the road leading to the bridge that the messenger, my next target, appears (come to disturb the order my bullets impose). Trudging along on the other side of the mountain, he wishes to bring hope to those who endure in the ruins I watch over. He wishes to inspire in them a new will to live (with neither food nor heat) in the icy cold amidst their shattered houses. To resist. To survive. Their overriding obsession. And even if the messenger comes with bad news (their parents have died tragically, their home town has been demolished, their women massacred) we have no need for such disinformation, no need for news that strays from the reality our propaganda defines. The messenger (if he isn't a scout dressed up as a peasant) will be my second victim today, after the madwoman who went to fetch some water (and after the officer yesterday morning, and the nurse from the Red Cross last night). Whether he is messenger or spy, all I see is the amazement in his eyes as he is struck in the face by a bolt of lightning come from above (the sky being quite cloudless). Ah! The dead messenger (like all those troublemakers I've just described – and all the ones to come!) is a job well done. A dead messenger means no more disinformation, no more false rumours, no more twisting of reality!

6

On the road leading to the border, a long line of cars, tractors and buses snakes around trees struck down by mortar shells, burned-out vehicles, roadblocks set up to harass refugees, exploded landmine craters. The people are afraid. The border crossing is not far, but nothing (not until the last minute, not until they've taken their first steps on the land beyond the border) guarantees that they'll be lucky enough to escape from the soldiers and their harassment, cross the border and set foot (after days on the road) in the neighbouring country. Exhausted, they still hear air-raid warnings, see their villages in ruins, think of the dead stretched out on the ground, smell the smoke coming from burning barns. Covered in old blankets and plastic sheets to keep out the cold and rain, they clutch water canisters and bags full of food, afraid of going hungry, afraid of drinking water from a poisoned well. A few hundred yards from the border, soldiers start flagging vehicles down. Buses, tractors, wheelbarrows and people on foot are to stay to the left, cars must keep to the right. On each side of the road, a line of policemen and soldiers contain and direct the flow, beat the refugees with their rifle butts. 'Move along, scum!' A group of thirty, without tractors or horses, are on foot. They have managed to make their way around roads ploughed up by bombs, get bearings in the smoke and mist, avoid roadblocks where soldiers strip-search the women for money and jewels. They have seen dozens of buses under police escort pass by, horse-drawn carts, people on bicycles, trailers crammed with suitcases and clothes, shepherds on donkeys fleeing across the fields, peasants who prefer to take the mountain paths rather than the mined roads. A bus stops at the border checkpoint. Some soldiers board, point out a group of men. 'Get off the bus, you're under arrest!' A patrol watches the operation, guns pointed at the people left on the bus. The arrested men are silent. What can they do, empty handed as they are, with assault rifles aimed at them? In the same line, having just arrived at the border after a hundred miles on the road, a trailer is brought to a halt. 'Your papers!' An old man lowers his head, an old woman raises her arms. 'Have pity!' The soldiers load their guns without a word. 'Here are the papers,' says the man sitting at the steering wheel. The soldiers' chief looks at the papers. 'How many are you?' 'There are five of us.' The officer approaches the trailer, ostentatiously rips the papers up, ignores the old man's cries of protest, his gaze falling on the young girl hiding in her mother's arms. 'How old are you?' Her mother, staring straight in front of her, holds the child even more tightly to her breast. She would answer for her daughter, only since leaving her village she no longer speaks; the young man who rushed out of the house with his hunting rifle the day the soldiers arrived (and who, immediately afterwards, collapsed to the ground, riddled with bullets) was father to her child. Since the murder, she has remained in a silence peopled by bloody arms and legs and the charred ruins of the village where she was born, living only for her daughter. 'Let us go,' cries the old woman, trying to distract the officer's attention. 'We've seen enough dead!' 'What are you talking about?' the officer asks. 'You've seen dead people? Where? Your old head is full of dreams.' 'She knows what she's talking about,' says the man at the steering wheel. 'People killed by machine-gun fire, women raped, the village destroyed, she's seen all this.' 'You, get out of the tractor,' the officer says. The soldiers drag the man from his seat, prod his chest with their guns. 'So you say you've seen crimes?' The man turns his head away. 'Leave me alone, I'm innocent.' The soldiers' chief points at the girl, huddled in her mother's arms. 'Here, no one is innocent, except for her, maybe.' The mother hides her daughter under the blanket. The officer's voice grows louder. 'But she's too young to testify to your supposed innocence. However, her mother…' He pulls out his revolver. '…she could!' The soldiers snicker. 'Yes, let the mute one swear to this prick's innocence.' The officer puts his revolver to the man's forehead. 'You've given me false papers, you bastard. But if this woman (who I suspect is your sister) says you're innocent, I'll let you cross the border, despite your lies.' The soldiers groan. 'Declare him innocent!' 'Too easy!' 'Someone else must corroborate this!' The old woman stands up in the trailer. 'Her daughter's father was shot before her very eyes, leave her alone.' The soldiers stop laughing. 'You, shut the fuck up! As for her, if her brother's clean, she'll say so. Otherwise, she'll see him die.' '...and her daughter shafted,' says a drunken soldier. The officer waves the drunkard away. 'No one touches the little one!' He pulls down the trailer's side railing, holds out his hand for the little girl to take. 'Come here!' Mother and daughter clutch at each other, trembling. 'Come,' says the officer softly. 'She doesn't want you,' says a soldier with a bitter smile. The officer clasps his fingers around the back of the young girl's neck. 'Come here.' And with the swiftness of a predator sure of his prey, he wrenches the girl out of her mother's arms. 'Young girls like you shouldn't be allowed to leave this country.' While the officer leads the girl off to a van behind the border checkpoint, the soldiers restrain the other family members. 'Don't move!' The mother tries to get down from the trailer; the soldiers beat her back with their rifle butts. 'Stay where you are!' The officer locks the girl in the van, comes back to the trailer. 'Bring the mother over here.' The soldiers carry out the order. The officer grabs the mute one by the hair and turns her head towards the man surrounded by soldiers. 'Don't worry about your daughter. Better spare a thought for your brother. He gave us false papers. If you don't clear him, he's dead.' Grimacing desperately, the mute one digs her fingers deep into the rough fabric of the officer's uniform. 'Well?' the officer yells. 'Tell the truth! Is he innocent?' The mute one stares at him wide eyed. 'You won't speak. You send your brother to his grave!' The soldiers push the brother against a pillar supporting the border checkpoint roof. A volley of machine-gun fire fells him. 'There you are, you've got what you wanted,' the officer bellows. The mute one faints. 'And now, they'd better get out of here, or else they'll all get it!' The soldiers throw the mute one into the trailer, poke the old man in the ribs with their rifles. 'You, drive!'

7

The women standing in a line by the wall in HQ head office have straightened up, obedient to the commander who, now satisfied with their new improved postures, points at an officer. 'Tell us about your experience as a private, before you got promoted!' The officer steps out of the line. 'I cannot, commander.' The commander puts his hand on the officer's shoulder. 'Tell everybody here what you've been through, otherwise those new stripes on your uniform won't be there much longer!' The officer stares at the commander's boots. 'Two months in the trenches, not a single woman. Two months of life up to my neck in ripped-off legs, mangled bodies, bellies torn open by mortar shells, guts splattered all over the ground, arms raised to the heavens, human torsos dancing a terrifying csárdás of death: when a bullet hits a body running towards a trench where it seeks cover, it breaks the momentum in such a way as to produce contortions that no dancer could ever have imagined. Starts, pirouettes, jolts, twists of a horribleness which only death (when it strikes all of a sudden) can produce.' The commander walks up and down before the lined-up women, gets off on the emotion which electrifies their flesh. 'Two months in the trenches, not a single woman. Did you masturbate?' The officer frowns. 'I wanted to masturbate in front of a dead nurse, killed in an ambush. Common practice in the trenches, a practice held in high esteem among soldiers – but I preferred to rape her instead! Just before I came (her body was still warm), I felt she was coming back to life, so powerfully did I thrust inside her, so swollen was my prick. I left her there by the trench, my come mixing with her blood. I came back the next day, my fly undone. War, lopped-off arms and legs, the dead, vanquished cities lying in ruins, spur us on to coitus. To sow his seed in the midst of burned fields, to masturbate when there's no more flesh to rape, that's all a soldier thinks of.' The commander scrutinises the other officers. 'Have you understood? War leaves no one unscathed!' He turns back to the officer who has just described his experiences as a grunt. 'Which of these girls would you like to interrogate?' The officer points out a blonde. 'That slag there.' The commander looks the girl up and down. 'This one? Good choice.' He runs his hand through the girl's hair, pulls her head back, sticks a finger into her mouth, moves it slowly in and out. 'Tell us what happened to you before you were brought here!' The girl is silent. 'Tell us,' says the commander. 'Or do you need some reminding?' The girl sees the commander move his hand down between her legs, wants to avoid being penetrated once again. 'Our bus was stopped at a roadblock. The minute I saw soldiers coming, I escaped. Through a smashed window at the back of the bus. The soldiers made the driver get out. I saw their torches slicing through the night. Women were screaming and crying. I ran back up the road to get away from the roadblock. Before I could jump into a ditch, the soldiers' dogs started barking. Three soldiers gave chase. They knocked me to the ground. I was holding a rock in each hand, but I didn't defend myself. I didn't want them to kill me. The following evening, after the soldiers had again raped me in their van, I was taken to prison. There was someone else in the torture chamber. They locked me up in the next room. Through the partition I could see what was going on there. At first I didn't understand. A woman on her hands and knees, at the mercy of a huge dog behind her, was moving her head up and down in front of an officer. And while the dog's claws tore her back, her tormentor shoved his phallus (so swollen it had taken on that purple colour of flesh about to explode) into her mouth. The soldier guarding me (me, fresh meat) exulted, seeing the expression on my face. Nothing excites these demons more than the terror a woman feels when she discovers what is to become of her!' The commander lets the girl go. 'You've learned to tell your story well…too well, perhaps!' He pushes her towards the officer who chose her. 'Take this bitch to the torture chamber. I'd like to know whether she has other tales to tell!'

8

Out of breath, his arms and legs trembling, the man looks at the frozen ground. This mix of stone, clods, mud and decomposing twigs is harder and more compact than concrete. The messenger was right. The village was burned. Nor is there any trace of either his parents or his brothers. Though they must be here somewhere. Somewhere in this earth, whose stubborn refusal to yield itself up is killing him (he thinks). The pick and spade are useless. His nails break. With his steel-capped boots he kicks in vain. He breathes in the frozen air. Anger rises up through his chilled body. Like the heat from a blacksmith's forge, it spreads out from his stomach to his fingertips; warms the muscles up, sets his cheeks and temples aflame. The most frozen part of his brain (the part that froze up on seeing the village of his birth) has come back to life. He has found the houses burned. He has walked through the charred fields. And he has found not a living person. He has found none of the dead either. Nevertheless he is quite sure (as the messenger hinted) that they are all here. But where? He has started to look for them again. He has come to a place in a field where the earth has recently been turned over. He has tried to dig. But the earth, so frozen over that it resists pick and spade better than a block of concrete, refuses to open up. He looks at his hands. If the earth refuses to open up, it is because it hides in its guts of ice those he is looking for. He stands, exhausted by this futile attempt at digging. He is throwing in the towel before having broken through that crust of ice. He is not dead yet. Though he is seeking the dead. And in grasping this, he is driven to the brink of madness. Man without reason. Man who has lost the faculty of speech and discernment. The pick in his trembling hands confirms this failure. No, he repeats to himself. The smell of the earth, which rises up into his nostrils, reminds him he is alive. He needs to get his strength back. His struggle is not yet finished. The earth refuses to yield to him (despite the blows from the pick, despite the constant thrust of the spade), but this refusal on the earth's part to let him find the dead he has come for is like an insult which brings him back to life. He would rather drop dead, crashing amid the stones, than abandon the task he has set himself. He throws the pick away, sticks his frozen fingers into his mouth, sucks the tips to warm them up and taste the earth, this earth he once knew so well, in his childhood. Isn't it just a few dozen yards away that he saw for the first time human blood flowing? An accident in the field, farm machinery, he can't quite recall the circumstances, but he remembers clearly the red liquid that flowed from the wounded body, the peasant lying on the ground, clutching at the earth, breathing more and more rapidly, dying as his lifeblood flowed out of the gash: his heart sliced open by the spinning blade. Right now, the earth is so hard that the pick cannot smash through this armour of stones and mud, twigs and leaves. He lets out a roar. The axe. He must get the axe. No other instrument can slice through this barrier of ice that separates him from the dead he has come looking for. With blows from his axe he will open up this earth. Expose its guts. Release those it has imprisoned. For he well knows (even on the brink of madness) that he must break through this crust of ice now (while arctic temperatures destroy the survivors and wipe out all traces of what has happened); because in springtime, when the sun and the thaw come (those joyful harbingers of the first buds), such a change in temperature will remove all trace of blood and take away what remains of the dead. The earth, become an earth of ice, conceals the horror that has taken place. And pitilessly it cares nothing for his powerlessness in finding the dead. In making sure once and for all about that which he fears the most – that his family has gone. Anger blurs his sight. The blood thrums in his ears. But at the same time as he loses his reason and sense of discernment, he no longer hesitates. His body gains strength. With greater firmness his hand grasps the axe handle. Now that he is fully recovered, he sees nothing, neither the earth nor the block of ice beneath him, nor the winter sky nor the light reflected in the grey stones, but his resolve is of steel: muttering a few incomprehensible curses (damned earth) he raises the axe.

9

They say it's a cruel time? Violent? Despicable? I am pure violence. Given, however, that I am only obeying orders (to kill whoever threatens our empire), I am also above all moral considerations. Pure violence knows no criteria. It erupts. Kills. Annihilates. The incarnation of pure violence, I am myself the time. So shut up! Keep your traps drooling moral imperatives shut until one of my bullets shatters your cranium! Beyond the vile, I serve the state. To shoot those who are at work dismantling it is my duty. I aim, I execute – all those harmful to our regime. I have no preferences. No priorities. Soldiers, peasants, women, children, the old, doesn't matter. I do my job. And heads explode. Do I shoot people such as myself? Born a normal man, I learned (unlike my targets) conformity with the architects of order. The state foremost. Just a while back, I saw a group of people emerging from the ruins. They were exhausted, starving. Oh, joy! The suffering, the distress wrought on their faces, was due to my work. One of the women at the head of the group waved a white blouse. 'Let us leave the city.' I pulled the trigger. Her head exploded before the stunned group's very eyes. There you go! Only the mighty are safe in this world. While the meek…watermelons fit for the splattering! Who wants to kill the mighty anyway? Let's be realistic! If I start killing the mighty, who's going to supply the ammunition? Who pay me? Who's going to deliver new weapons? Being born is one thing, living is another. What do these dissident pigs want? That our state should fall? Their brains revolt me. They spatter the walls of houses, drip from the branches of trees the state planted along our city's avenues to improve the environment. Stupid idiots, retarded tossers! Dreams of power and material comfort haunt their skulls. They forget (soused to the gills on enemy propaganda) the sacrifices our regime made in nurturing them. Where is their rejection of diktats imposed by foreign powers? Where is their contempt for the materialistic filth that enemy capital floods us with? The populace wants what it doesn't deserve. Money without work. Honours without merit. I hate this vermin more than anything, because they infect our society, undermine the state, sabotage our regime. And men capable of flying our race's flag are ever rarer. Look around you. In this city, traitors and profiteers dream of the enemy regime's wealth, ready to accept its domination. There's an entire army of parasites out there, decked out in rags to stir pity in the hearts of foreign observers. Help us. Subsidise our development. Born in our land but ready to collaborate, they are waiting for the enemy regime to come here as master. But our state will defend itself. Those

I kill are the embryos of a society of arrogance and profit (a despicable, vile and contemptible society) which a few of us are still around to reject. The enemy wants to annihilate our state to complete its empire. It sows in our land the seeds of that imported filth which is devouring cultures the world over. In ten years, even here (if it's not resisted), our citizens will be members of another state, slaves to a universal mindlessness. While they deserve death.

10

The van parked beneath the roof of the border checkpoint starts up. After going past soldiers directing traffic, it slows down and the officer (alone at the wheel, the girl locked up in the back) yells, 'Move the scum out, I'll be back in an hour.' The soldiers, forcing a passage through that sea of vehicles blocking the road, salute their superior. 'Don't worry, we'll get things moving.' 'See you later, chief!' The van passes between tractors loaded with refugees, takes the road leading to the forest. One of the soldiers, seeing the officer's van disappearing into the trees, spits on the ground. 'The bastard, he's going to fuck the little one. As for us…all we're good for is the dirty work.' 'Don't be an arsehole,' says another soldier. 'When's he's not around we're cool. Don't you remember how many bitches you shafted yesterday?' 'He's right,' says a third soldier. 'When he's away, no one breaks our balls. I don't mind getting my oar in either now and then.' 'Anyway, let's go see the next pack of tossers that's arrived.' The soldiers flag down a tractor at the head of a column of refugees. 'Show us your papers!' Checking in his rear-view mirror to see the line of tractors moving, the officer smiles contentedly. 'If I didn't let that gang of crooks poke some refugee bitches, they'd refuse to work!' The van disappears into the forest. The officer pulls back the panel in the driver's compartment, adjusts the rear-view mirror. 'You a virgin?' The girl, huddled up in the back, hides her head in her lap. 'I know what girls your age are like,' the officer murmurs. 'Only yesterday, we came across a girl hardly older than yourself. She was already a whore. When I told her to get undressed, she said, "I love sodomy!" She got down on her knees, wanted to suck me, lick my balls, swallow my come. I kicked her away. "Slag!" My soldiers fucked her one after the other. She thought that if she took it up the arse we'd let her go. "Shove it in!" she said. I gave the order to slash her belly open, pull out that adder's nest she had for guts, throw them to the dogs. But you, I can see you're pure. That's why I'm taking you elsewhere.' A bunker appears in the middle of some dunes, a concrete cube hemmed in by the forest and the barbed-wire fence that marks the border. The van avoids mounds of bushes, the wheels spin as it climbs a sandy slope – the brakes bring the steel hulk to a halt a few yards from the bunker. The officer goes round to the back of the van, opens the doors, drags the girl out. 'See that entrance there? Let's go!' The girl obeys, and then, sensing that the officer is not following too close behind, runs towards the dunes. The officer, who has been dreaming of this flight, watches her pubescent girl's legs, her waist, her hair floating in the wind. These desperate efforts arouse in him emotions he has longed to feel. Struggling up the steep slope, the young girl falls before reaching the top of the dune, rolls back down to where the officer is standing at the bottom of the slope. 'Dirty little bitch, don't you know how to obey?' He pushes the girl back to the ground, pins her arms down with his knees, sticks his cock in her mouth. 'Don't you realise that if you want me to let you go you first have to satisfy my wishes?' The officer sinks his fingers into the girl's hair, frantically moves her head back and forth, shoving his cock deep into her mouth as he climaxes. 'You see?' he whispers into the girl's ear. 'It's much better to be nice!' But instead of quieting down, the girl, the minute her legs are free, knees her aggressor in the jaw. A fierce pain blinds the officer. He brings his hand to his mouth, feels his rammed upper and lower teeth. His tongue hangs, a string of bloody meat. 'Miserable whore!' he splutters, spitting blood. The girl gives him another kick, manages to get up, tries to make for the dunes again; but before she can completely get away, the officer, skewered with pain, grabs her. 'Dirty slapper, I'm going to slaughter you!' Dragged by the hair towards the bunker, the girl struggles, tries to bite her assailant's arms, but he doesn't seem to feel her clawing at him. Inside the bunker, he ties his prey, arms and legs splayed, to the four pillars supporting the roof, rips off her dress, and stands before her naked body, which nothing (except a pair of urine-stained knickers) protects. 'You wanted to kill me?' Forgetting his pain, the officer bends down over the breasts, scratches the skin around the areolae, bites the nipples, then moves down towards the spread thighs, offered up to his bestial instincts. When he realises that the blood dropping on her pubescent girl's belly comes from his own mouth, he lets out a scream, rips off the urine-stained knickers, plunges his head between the spread thighs, opens the vagina, and sticks his tongue in the slit, gives it a few exploratory licks, pulls his head back to locate the clitoris. The girl's body contracts, but the ropes fastened to the pillars tighten ever more painfully around her wrists and ankles. On his knees before the spread thighs, the officer watches the teenager's spasms, then lowers his head to excise the clitoris, but before he can sink his teeth into the flesh a length of metal wire is around his neck. The mute one, at the head of a group of fugitives, drags him backwards. He lets go of the girl, tries to grab at the wire strangling him, loses his balance, tries not to fall, kicks out at the intruders who have crept into the bunker – but the mute one, the wire wrapped tight around her hands protected with pieces of cloth, is pulling like a rabid bitch. 'Die, murderer!' someone shouts. The mute one sends the officer crashing to the ground, the metal wire bursts the arteries – out of the huddle of fugitives a hand appears holding a knife. 'Finish him off!' the mute one seems to scream. While one of the fugitives sinks the knife into the officer's throat, the mute one gives the metal wire to another woman and, hoping it's not too late, rushes to her daughter. The ropes that tie the girl to the pillars are sliced. As the mute one holds her daughter in her arms, a bloody hand holds out a piece of meat. 'It's the bastard's heart, eat it.' The mute one sinks her teeth into the meat, tears off a piece which she then swallows, then hands the remains of the organ to the others. After tossing it on to the officer's mutilated body, the fugitives leave the bunker. The mute one points at the van. 'Search it,' a woman interprets. Two men go through the vehicle, rummage in every corner, come back with a bayonet and an iron bar. The mute one points towards the forest. 'Let's go!' shouts a man. The fugitives, wrapped up in blankets and winter coats, armed with weapons stolen from the van, set off towards the forest.

11

The commander walks before the line of women, chooses ones who, as his officers stand to attention, he kicks to the ground. 'Who wants her?' The officers are silent. 'No one?' The commander nervously taps his thigh. 'I do,' says one of the officers finally. 'Good,' says the commander, smiling. 'Go fetch the prisoners we're interrogating today.' The officer goes out of the room. The other officers, wary and stiff, look at the woman at their feet. 'What's your opinion?' the commander asks. 'Is she slut enough? Would you rather she had fewer clothes on?' The door of HQ opens again. Five prisoners, in dirty camouflage, faces covered in cuts and bruises, enter. 'Stand there, backs against the wall!' the commander orders. Once the order has been carried out, the commander studies the prisoners. 'Do you know what your women can expect if you refuse to tell us where your accomplices are hiding?' With a wink, he gives the officer who expressed his wish to possess the woman permission to proceed. 'A demonstration!' The officer pushes the woman on to her hands and knees, kneels behind her, grabs her by the hair, pulls her head back so she can see the prisoners. 'Are you ready?' Violently penetrated, the woman screams. 'Anyone want to talk?' the commander asks. The prisoners remain silent. The commander fells one with a kick in the testicles. Beaten by the officers, the man passes out. 'Nobody wants to talk?' The commander pulls out his revolver and shoots dead another prisoner. 'Tie one of those sluts to the bed!' While the officers go about this, the commander sits on the dead body. 'You're in my power here,' he screams at the prisoners. 'Your lives aren't even worth one of my cigarette butts! Where are your weapons? Where are the other fighters? When do they plan to attack our position?' No one answers. 'Still nothing?' The commander picks out another prisoner, points with his gun at some pieces of brain and shattered skull on the floor. 'Pick that up.' Thrown to the floor by the officers, the prisoner puts the bloody fragments into the cup of his hand. 'Now stuff the bitch's mouth with it!' The woman, still trembling from the first assault she has been subjected to, swallows the pieces of bone and brain matter. 'No one's got the courage to speak?' The commander walks over to the woman tied to the bed, pensively contemplates her splayed legs, then gives his officers another order. 'Resuscitate the prisoner who passed out!' The officers come back from the flaming stove in the corner with a white-hot metal poker, press a gun against the head of the prisoner who picked up the pieces of brain and shattered skull, force him to take the instrument of torture. 'Wake your comrade up!' The white-hot poker burns the unconscious prisoner's feet. He lets out a terrible scream. The commander waits until the smell of burning flesh fills the room at HQ, then points at the woman on the bed. 'Rape her!' While the officers undo their flies, the commander studies the prisoner burned so badly there is bone sticking out of his foot. 'Now some motor oil!' A bottle full of motor oil is pushed down the burned man's throat. 'No one got their memory back?' the commander enquires. 'No one,' the officers reply. 'Where's the one who likes torturing his comrades?' The officers point out the prisoner who is into torture. 'You don't remember where the others are either?' The prisoner grits his teeth. With his forefinger, the commander points at the vagina of the woman splayed on the bed, out of which dribbles – now that the officers have all climaxed – a gob of come. 'Disinfect the slut!' The officers push the barrel of a gun against the prisoner's temple. 'Understand?' The prisoner doesn't move. Safety mechanisms click. 'Go on,' the officers order. 'Shove it up her!' The prisoner grits his teeth, pushes the poker between the woman's legs, falls in a dead faint on top of her. 'Where's the one who drank the motor oil?' the commander yells. The officers point at the motor oil drinker, tied to a leash like a fighting dog. 'Still suffering from defective memory? Select a comrade to talk for you.' The officers go over to one of the prisoners standing with his back to the wall and slash open his trousers. 'This one?' The commander points at the man's testicles. 'Tear them off.' The prisoner whimpers. 'Didn't you hear?' the soldiers' chief says with some impatience. A burning torch sets fire to the motor oil running out of the captive's rectum. 'Tear them off!' the officers scream. The fighting dog sinks its jaws into the genitals. 'Kill him,' the commander concludes. 'Can't you see he's gone mad?' The officers shoot the demented man. 'Now tie one of these cunts to my work desk!' the commander says. The officers pick out a woman, take her to the table, tie her arms and legs up. The commander yells at the surviving prisoners: 'Pack of bastards, I'll make you talk! Where are your arms dumps? Where are your accomplices? What do they plan to do?' Then, angered by the prisoners' silence, he bears down on the woman tied to the table, positions himself between her legs, grabs hold of her breasts, lets out a roar, and, with an enraged thrust, pierces her flesh.

12

The axe blade clangs off a stone, slices through a frozen branch, pierces the ice: tiny lumps of topsoil spatter his face, a block of ice flies off, and, in a crack between two lumps of earth, his father's face appears, mouth and eyes wide open. The man draws back. His old father looks him straight in the eyes with a gaze full of horror. Pain and rage distort his face, a terrible grimace of horrified rejection of what he saw at the moment (so the son thinks) when the soldier shot him; his wife dead, his two sons dying, and he himself (the father) the last one standing, overwhelmed by rage and by a feeling of unbearable injustice. The father must have felt this since the mortars hit the village and the drunken soldiers, swaggering with their power, drove the people from their homes. To flee, stray across the fields, hide in the forest, wander over the snow-covered mountains, this was their fate now; this manhunt in which they were the hunted sank the old man into despair, and his son (how many days later?) can see this despair, still there, in the eyes of his father who, from between the two lumps of earth, looks at him. The man raises the axe. More earth loosens beneath the coat of ice, pebbles fly up, the frozen armour is finally beginning to give way, and one of his old father's arms (thrown up to protect him from the bullets flying towards his chest) rises out of the ground. The man climbs into the hole his axe has dug, pulls out two large stones. He will have to pull many more from off his father's chest (riddled with bullets) to reveal completely his terrible gaping wound (black around the edges, red by the heart), which seems still to bleed, despite the thick layer of frost that the arctic cold has spread over it. The sight of his father's body ripped open causes him to drop the axe. He starts walking around the hole, slips in ruts, stumbles across stones and lumps of clay, stamps the ground with the heel of his steel-capped shoes. What else does this blood-drenched earth hide? The freezing air doesn't bring down the fever that has taken hold of him. Fucking war! As the earth he walks across in rising fever begins to shift, the smell of death rises out of the hole; heavy, stomach-churning death floats in the air, rises up through his nostrils, aggravates his nerves, while all around him, beneath his feet which stamp and smash the ice, human remains start to emerge: a hand with cut-off fingers slips out of a hole, a leg bone rises out of the cracked coat of ice, a jaw spits dead leaves, and shreds of fabric (mixed with burned grass) tell of a dozen dead people's burned clothes. The man stops, looks around him, then, remembering why he has come, he hurries towards the axe: if his father is here, then his mother and two brothers are also; and even though he will never see them alive again, he wants at least to bring up their bodies – and the corpses rising out of the earth around him (the murderers' unexpected allies) won't stop him! The murderers doubtlessly counted on such an alliance: the corpses, which confirm the horror of the crimes, cause even the bravest to shrink away; terror destroys even the firmest resolve. But in order to condemn such crimes, must they not be etched out in all their monstrosity? Otherwise everything (including the mass graves, the discovered victims, the burned flesh) works in favour of the murderers. To dig, hammer at the earth where these crimes are hidden, is the only way to find out what has happened – since ignorance, absence of any proof, and refusal to uncover what has taken place are to the murderers' advantage. Letting out an animal groan, the man picks up the axe, strikes once, then strikes again and again. The axe blade, falling regularly on the piled-up stones (the better to entomb the victims in their graves), sends sparks flying. In the depth of winter, which all day long sinks the earth into darkness, he needs one of these tiny lamps to light the hole that, as the axe falls, opens up in the earth (the hole dug in the frozen earth out of which the dead will come).

13

Who can find me here, in my hiding place, the concrete entrance to the underground gallery? Scouts, fighter jets? A drone's idiot eye? I keep watch. Disobedience is our greatest enemy. Even before the air raids began, the screw hadn't tightened enough. My first fit of rage (which I remember perfectly) came one day (in spring) when subversive elements began tearing down our regime's monuments. At the time, orders weren't clear. Should we intervene? Brutally stamp out? Bide our time? Preserve a veneer of civic peace? Seeing these bandits attack our regime's symbols, I seized the initiative. The state is never severe enough. Its army can never be repressive enough with those who go on the offensive. I loaded my gun. What else did you expect? I shot for the first time. The thug who had raised a hammer to signal an attack against the state dropped dead. Spitting blood. Amazed that the monument he had wanted to bludgeon to bits still had the power to kill. Die, you rioter! His eyes bulging, his mug face down in the muck, the dissident suffered his final agonies. No doubt he wished to offer up a few last terms of abuse, but all he could do was whine. The squeals a pig makes when its throat is cut gurgled up out of his bubbling mouth. First to raise a hammer against the state, first to drop dead with a broken skull! Fair? The state must defend itself, so history shows. There are always individuals (from all social strata) that good old anti-state propaganda first leads astray from the true path then brings to the ranks of parasites ready to lift their hammers against the state. In truth, these dissident elements have nothing to propose except to smash up statues, bring down what the state has built up, destroy symbols of the regime under whose wing they (drunks, dirt merchants, debauchees, drug addicts, queers) all vegetate. I shot several times again, picked off three other bandits who had dared attack our monuments. Soon these sons of bitches were in their thousands, hammering away at the concrete, unscrewing the bolts that fastened our statues to their stone plinths, sawing at the structures of the state. Give these insubordinate elements a bit of room to operate, and your regime starts crumbling at the foundations, beginning with your monuments! After neutralising a dozen rioters, I needed to reload my rifle. My ammunition! All run out…in peacetime you can never think enough about arming yourself. What's a sniper without cartridges? A poor fucker who looks on helplessly as the state is taken to pieces. Full of wrath, I screamed: The arms industry is the cornerstone of every state! To aim without being able to shoot (his magazine empty) is death for a sniper! The beginning of the regime's dissolution!

In the meantime, concrete panels fell away from the plinths under attack, the monuments trembled in the city overwhelmed by rioters, the marble succumbed to the rage of hammers, while I (powerless and frustrated) waited for the next delivery of ammunition. They were many to take advantage of the state's weakness! The first statue fallen, the arm of a second one flung heavenward, the third one unsteady on its legs, I could not intervene (and put a stop to this sorry spectacle) until the next crate of ammunition arrived. Are you honest citizens? To fight for our regime's survival is a duty! I reloaded my gun. Fire! Fire! One rioter dead. Two more snuffed out. Fire again! The final result? Instead of watching our regime fall, I watched rioters fall instead, their hopes of bringing down our state reduced to spurts of brain.

14

Slipping, unsteady, the fugitives trudge along the muddy forest trail left by tank tracks and wheels of army trucks. If they want to get closer to the border, there is no alternative; the forest, however, is so dense, the mountain slopes so steep, that to clamber over fallen tree trunks, beat a way through brambles, stay clear of cliff drops, lift feet sucked down by the marshy ground, is almost too much to ask of these men and women exhausted by days and days of flight. And even if they do manage to reach the mountain summit and get down the other side, the border will still be a long way off, the terrain still hostile, and it is crucial they make it across the border (which pass they take matters little) before the first snows. The mute stops at a crossroads. Most of the army trucks (at least the tanks, judging by the tracks) turned right, probably towards a military base. The lighter vehicles turned left. Towards a border checkpoint? The mute one looks at her companions. Dirty, shivering with the cold, they appear to be at the end of their tether. The mute one points doubtfully at the trail going off to the left. 'Let's go this way,' says the man, nodding. But the fugitives don't move. 'Why don't we stay here while you check out the terrain?' suggests a woman, speaking for the exhausted members of the group. The mute one shakes her head. 'We have to stick together,' says the man, backing her up. 'If we separate, nothing guarantees we'll find each other again.' The fugitives set off at a slow pace on the trail leading off to the left, leaving behind the tank tracks. Puddles, mounds of mud that the trucks threw up, crushed branches, bracken, loose stones make the walk difficult. Soaked, chilled, the fugitives walk more and more slowly. The grey sky weighs heavily on their bowed backs, the darkness increases their fears. As they come out of a turn (the road descending between two rocky outcrops) the mute one (who up till now has been walking a few dozen yards ahead) comes to a stop. The man and the girl catch up with her. The other fugitives remain rooted to the spot. If they have to turn back, every step forward is a step lost, and no one has the energy to start playing scout. The mute one points out a farmhouse roof. The man surveys the area, notices smoke rising into the sky, breathes the air. 'Smells of burning,' he says. 'Better check the place out, see who lives here, but be very careful.' 'I'll go,' the girl cries. The mute one grabs her arm. 'Stay with your mother,' says the man. 'I'll go.' He moves away from the group, becomes a shadow sliding along the tree trunks, disappears completely into the foliage. A few minutes later, a sharp whistle signals the all-clear. 'Come on,' cries the girl. 'We've found somewhere to stay!' The fugitives press forward. The mists that haunt this borderland forest disperse as they come to a clearing, where the farm stands. As the fugitives get closer to the farmhouse and its adjoining outbuilding (in an L shape), the smell of burning, mixed with the acrid stink of slaughtered animals, grows more oppressive. From the farmhouse roof, mostly fallen in, a column of smoke climbs skyward, whipped by flames that leap out of the ruins. The house was looted – the soldiers pushed front door, furniture, crockery and a framed family photograph into the middle of the sitting room, broke and smashed everything, doused it all in petrol – and a lighter, having no doubt served to light a cigarette, set the lot on fire. Slaughtered horses, cows blown to bits, dogs shot in the head and chickens with their throats cut lie scattered around the farm. In several places the slogan 'Death to half-breeds' covers walls smeared with excrement and blood. But there are no human remains to be found among the animal cadavers. Did the farm's inhabitants have time to escape? No mass grave can be seen in the pasture behind the stables, no telltale garment floats in the slurry pit, no dunghill has recently been moved. The mute one sees that the fugitives have filled a pail of water from the well in the garden; she gestures wildly, manages to get the man's attention; but just at the moment he understands why she is gesticulating, a woman takes a sip of the lukewarm water. 'Don't drink!' the man cries. But the woman gulps the water down. Before she can hand the bucket over to another fugitive, she doubles up, lets go of the pail, clutches her throat and falls to the ground. 'Don't touch either the water or the food,' the man yells. The fugitives gather around the woman racked by spasms, look on powerless at her agony. Nothing can be done to help her, no antidote can stop the crippling pain. The men curse heaven, the women burst into tears, cry, until the girl, who has disappeared, comes out of the stables shouting, 'Help, they're all here!' The fugitives, frightened, start running towards the forest. The mute one and the man give chase, the mute one gesticulating, the man yelling, 'Don't be afraid, she didn't mean soldiers!' Once the fugitives have come back, the man gathers them around the fire. 'Dry your clothes and try to get warm, we'll go and see what she's found!' The mute one and the man go into the stable. Through the half-open door, some light penetrates the stable's interior, makes visible the members of the family who used to live on the farm. Disembowelled, hung up by the feet like beasts in a slaughterhouse, they swing back and forth in the half-light. 'Killed by the soldiers,' says the man. The mute one clenches her fists. After a moment of hopelessness, they search the stable. 'There's nothing to eat, nothing to drink,' the man says. 'Do you think we could roast one of the dead animals in the yard?' The mute one hesitates, then shrugs as though to say yes. The man sighs. 'What else can we do? We've got to eat and drink. We'll roast something, and I'll send someone down to the cellars to have a look. There might be a bottle or two of something.' They go back to the fugitives gathered round the fire. 'There's nothing to be afraid of,' says the man. 'The girl just made a mistake. It was only...' The mute one glares. 'Scarecrows?' the girl cries. The mute one holds her so tightly in her arms she muffles her sobs. 'Bales of hay and scarecrows back from the fields after harvest is done,' says the man, the only one to laugh at his rural turn of phrase. The mute one gestures, shows the fugitives sitting around the fire the stairway leading down to the cellar. 'We've got to drink something,' says the man. 'The well's been poisoned. The water in the trough stinks. Who wants to go down and see if there isn't a stock of booze somewhere?' With night starting to fall, the fugitives are drying their clothes still; they eat roast meat and drink plum brandy found in the cellar, put another log on the fire. Suddenly the mute one stands up. 'I can hear motors,' says the woman next to her. The fugitives jump up. A dull rumbling, which the fugitives can distinguish from a thousand other noises, heralds the arrival of army trucks. 'Follow me,' says the man. 'We'll take the path behind the stables, escape through the forest before the trucks arrive!'

15

The officer pushes the woman into the cellar reserved for special interrogations. 'Get in, slut!' A metal ladder, fixed to the floor and ceiling, stands in the centre of the room. The officer locks the door. 'Look at what's in store for you!' The woman sees blood and semen stains, spots a bloody dress hanging from the back of the only chair in the room, turns her gaze away from a bra and a pair of knickers in shreds. Scattered all over the floor, chains, army belts, ropes, clubs, knuckle-dusters and baseball bats suggest the sort of interrogation that takes place here. The woman's anxiety grows as she notices a crate (recently delivered so as to widen the variety of available instruments of torture) full of assorted weapons and tools: batons, cables, barbed wire, belts, dildos, arrows, hammers, broken bottles, ammunition belts, bayonets, saws. 'Up against the ladder,' the officer commands. Straightening her back, pushing out her chest, the woman moves towards the ladder. 'You don't need to tie me up,' she says, on seeing the straps hanging from the rungs. The officer fastens her arms, rips her dress, grabs her breasts. 'I don't need to tie you up?' 'No, I'll do anything you want!' The officer pushes the woman to her knees, adjusts the length of the straps, unbuttons his trousers. 'Are you sure?' The woman looks at the cock bulging out of the officer's trousers. 'Yes!' The officer wraps the woman's hair around his wrist, brandishes his cock before her mouth. 'You're a real whore!' The woman smiles. 'Everyone is a whore when a good-looking guy overwhelms you.' The officer pales. The woman moves her head closer to his crotch. 'You can kill me, I'm yours.' The officer grips the woman's neck, smears his cock along the flesh of her lips, then shoves it deep into her throat. 'Suck, slapper!' The woman sucks, feels the cock swell in her mouth, wraps her lips around the gland, licks along the throbbing vein, sucks faster, nibbles the tumescent flesh, sighs. 'Untie my hands, I want to cup your balls!' The officer smiles. 'Think you can scare me?' He unties the woman's hands. She takes hold of his testicles, tickles his member at the root, caresses the secretive balls, cups the scrotal sac, flutters her eyelids and starts sucking again: the regular movement back and forth of her blonde head makes the officer moan. 'Faster!' The woman obeys, then grabs the cock with her two hands. 'Stuff me!' The officer grunts. The slit glistening with juice (reflected in the mirror behind the ladder) looks like a mouth with saliva oozing out of it. 'Turn around,' he yells, shaking his machine gun at her. 'I want your arse!' The woman holds on to the machine gun barrel. 'My arse. OK.' A wave of excitement sweeps through the officer. 'And then…' '…your prick up my arse and the gun barrel up my cunt!' 'Huh?' 'Double penetration, double your bitch!' The officer whinnies. The woman leans back against the ladder, takes hold of his cock, wanks the hardened organ, watches with the look of a slut about her as her torturer grimaces, then (feeling his orgasm coming) she nudges the gun towards him, pushes his hands away and – a few seconds before his semen starts to spurt – pulls the trigger. 'Bastard!' Shot in the stomach, he reels. Blood and entrails spill out of the wound. She tries to tear the gun out of his hands, can't do it, sinks her teeth into the still-throbbing cock, tears off that piece of male flesh which refuses to go limp. 'You slag,' splutters the officer. Another round of gunfire resounds, the officer jerks, then, contorted by spasms, falls mangled to the floor. In the blink of an eye, the woman wrenches the gun out of his hands as he gasps in his final agony, shoots again, walks towards the door, retraces her steps and, with the heel of her shoe, gouges her torturer's eyes out. 'So you can see the people you murdered better!' And she leaves the cellar.

16

The hole dug out of the frozen earth is getting bigger. He's already up to his chest in it. Behind his sweating back, a heap of stones, clods and branches piles skyward. His father's body is already in the cart where (still in that attitude of a man resisting infamy, arm raised to protect himself from the bullets aimed at his chest) he watches his son dig. The son wanted to throw his jacket (or a cloth) over his head, so his father couldn't watch him digging; it annoyed him to feel he was being watched, he wanted no one to witness his struggle with the ice (a struggle whose outcome is more and more uncertain given that his arms are now weak and the palms of his hands are bleeding). Then, telling himself that he was alone anyway (the only living person in the bottom of this mass grave which no living person should have found), he decided not to: since then, his dead father, frozen in that attitude of a resistant unjustly condemned to an unjust death, supervises with eyes wide open his son's stubborn work in the mass grave, his son (being the only living person among the dead) no longer his son only: the son now of all the dead who await exhumation so they can scream their pain, he is the man who has accepted the task of pitting his strength (with nothing in his hands except an axe) against the frozen earth and stones. And by the same token to confront the horror of a crime perpetrated on this bit of earth which (like thousands of other bits of earth the world over) he would care nothing for but for the accident of his birth here. Right now, having struck hundreds of blows with the axe, he no longer thinks of what surrounds him (his father, the mound of stones, the dead risen from the earth), sees only the black earth, is conscious only of the fact that he is here to find the three other dead (his mother and two brothers) who must be somewhere here too. The axe blade rises, slices through a tree branch, an artery encrusted in the solid armour plating of mud which connects two blocks of frozen earth – and he drops the axe (his hands covered in blood) at the very moment this tombstone of clods and putrefying grass breaks beneath his feet and shatters into a thousand shards of muddy ice. His mother (murdered first because she screamed as the soldiers bore down upon them) lies contorted in the same pose as when the bullets (fired in bursts) crucified her. Revolted by this ignominious deed, she seems worried as to the fate of her two sons, a mother eternally devoted to her progeny, even in the face of her own death. Her two sons, which the bullets struck down immediately afterwards, the minute they tried to defend themselves: their bodies, riddled with bullets, testify to the high price they paid in seeking to resist the soldiers' attack and avenge their mother. Without the slightest hesitation, the soldiers then reloaded their rifles and emptied their magazines into bodies already dead: although they were dead, their revolt, their resistance to these murderous deeds, seemed to have made an indelible impression on the minds of soldiers incapable of killing (as they did the living) this heroic rejection of the crime, this uncompromising resistance to those who take up weapons to exterminate people, this impossibly human courage (empty-handed against machine guns) to fight the inhuman. One of the sons (his brothers) still holds a stone in his hand, the only weapon he could find to defy the machine-gun fire. An ordinary stone (tight in his fist) became in his murderers' eyes an unforgivable weapon, his murderers whose power (and sense of victory gained in waging war against civilians) was (with this stone) refused, denied, fought, rejected. His bloody hands quivering, he breathes deeply as he looks at these bodies torn from the bowels of the earth. All he has to do now is put his mother's and brothers' exhumed bodies on to the cart (there where the father is waiting for them, eyes wide open, arm raised to the heavens). The axe, lying at his feet, has become a piece of iron battered by stones: he has dropped it without realising that this tool fashioned by the blacksmith's hammer is now no more than a shapeless metal lump, covered in blood and scraps of skin. He climbs back down into the hole he has dug in the earth. His mother's body slides out between clumps of earth and shards of ice; he stands her up and then, holding her in his arms, lifts her out. The father, standing in the carriage, watches with eyes wide open (eyes now amazed and full of disbelief) as his wife (followed by his two sons) rises out of the bowels of the frozen earth which until now (in a way both unforgivable and unjustifiable) concealed these crimes, this injustice.

17

Now, as the ground shakes beneath bombs and the wheels of army trucks moving towards the front, I hear appeals to God from all sides. O heaven! Some are leaving it to God and fighter jets to wipe our regime out, others are waging war and slitting throats in the name of their sacred soil, while the victims, stuck in the rut of history, shriek in despair, 'God, stop the massacres!' But God lets it happen. He's not that well informed on scorched-earth policies, or summary executions, or deportations, or extermination camps, or the slaughter of civilians. As for the human community? The promises the foreign powers have been making (since the start of the conflict) extend to the Peace–Love–God trinity; while the threats fanatics utter rely on a slightly altered version of the same: God–Hate–War. For some the sacred cow is belief; for others the right to intervene where the exactions hold back the consolidation of their empire. And all call on God to bless their war. Their holy war. War on evil. And the dead? No one (no state) is a saint, but it's thanks to the intercession of the saints that the whole thing has come to a boil. The state has only one enemy – religion! Fanatics summon up the spectre of holy war the minute they've got the chance. Everywhere there are saints swarming. There are far too many (to avoid any more wars): our Church's saints, the turbanned saints over on the other side, and then the droves of recently canonised ones – Saint Oil, Saint Business, Saint Capital. They seethe, they rage, they pull the strings of history, and here am I (old-fashioned secular, clear-minded atheist) sent to do the dirty work. The reasons for this war, clear at the outset (when our politicos took to the podium, making us believe there were racial and religious differences), aren't so clear now. A new demarcation line, a new boundary, has been drawn right down the middle of humanity: on one side the last men, on the other HATE-FILLED MURDERERS and TECHNOCRATS, thirsting for vengeance, who don't exist without God, holy books, machines and capital. As for me (when waves of depression cloud my conscience) I feel I'm firing blindly. Squeezing a trigger isn't enough, power relations are the only reality. Without them, the moon wouldn't go round the earth, the earth round the sun. And bombs wouldn't fall on people's heads, revealing to them the laws of the universe. But I don't forget my duty. Shoot. Assassinate. Increase the body count. And as for the war's origins…Pah! For a few days now (from the moment I noticed that nothing was clear, that an obscure massacre plotted by the mighty has supplanted the planned project) I've been shooting with a fervour as deep as my desire to have my revenge on their schemes. Down with saints! To hell with religions! With a movement of the index finger, a tiny movement certainly, insignificant on a universal scale of things, I give you horror in its purest state. My bullets will show what the saints have been hiding! And if a million corpses aren't enough, then I'll keep shooting. Tremble, shithead saints! The index finger is man's most important digit. Some raise it (so as to reveal the divine presence above?) whereas I curl it round the trigger – and what I can reveal with a single squeeze goes far beyond the world's saints and their revelations! My index finger writes the history of humanity's final act, reveals what man has become. Those who survive might like to think about it (if the revelation doesn't blow their minds – which is not impossible, given the scale of the horror).

18

At the edge of the mountain plateau, the fugitives appear in the dawn light, standing between bushes bent so far by the wind that the tops touch the ground. Behind them, the forest braces itself and groans with each blast of the storm; before them the immensity of the mountain plateau they are going to have to cross. The mute one gazes at the horizon, then looks at the place the man is insistently pointing at. 'A refugee camp,' he shouts (his voice, muffled by the wind, is nearly inaudible). 'A recently abandoned one.' The fugitives start walking towards the camp. A canvas city, with makeshift shops and bazaars, improvised canteens and showers, has been built in the middle of the plateau, a shanty town for refugees, where (judging by what's left) a hellish struggle for life went on for several months. The soldiers built a sewage treatment system to make up for the lack of drinking water, set up four generators for the camp's electricity supply and a field hospital for emergency operations. Around the base, they put up prefabs, with four camp beds, a table, two or three chairs, and a metal locker in each one. Farther on, standing on concrete foundations, an edifice made out of corrugated metal was home to the camp's administration. On sunny days, clothes washed in big plastic tubs were set out to dry on clothes lines strung up between poles that held the shelters up, while before the field kitchen the refugees, always starving, lined up holding big metal bowls, eager to have them filled with crushed wheat, beans and yogurt. After the camp was abandoned, the administration building was dynamited – the windows blew out, the roof collapsed and the walls were burned. The empty shells of tractors and buses (seats ripped up, windows smashed, doors covered in vengeful slogans: Kill the bastards!) are left standing on a patch of land used (as the petrol burns on the grass show) as a parking area. Empty suitcases and travel bags, broken crutches and stretchers, prams and wheelchairs, plastic bags and sheeting lie strewn amid collapsed tents. Apart from a few run-over dogs, no rotting carcasses clutter the muddy camp. The fugitives trudge through the detritus, looking under chipboard panels, sifting through mounds of rubbish and tipped-over dustbins, taking whatever leftovers they can find. The camp was vast. The dump that's replaced it takes up even more space, a tremendous rubbish tip in the middle of mountains devoid of human life. And the camp itself (the fugitives are sure) is without life. No man sleeps under a bit of plastic sheeting, no woman is hiding under a mound of refuse, no child is left abandoned in a discarded basket. When the fugitives get to the edge of the rubbish dump, they see that, at the other end of the plateau, rising out of the weeds, there was recently a military airbase. Dozens of planes loaded with food and first-aid supplies must have touched down on the landing strip hurriedly built on the flattest part of the plateau; dozens of planes loaded with refugees must have taken off from this dusty earth, bound for cities that offered asylum; dozens of helicopters must certainly have lifted off from here and dropped food and weapons into the back country; only yesterday hundreds of crates cluttered the meadows as they waited to be loaded on to army trucks to be delivered to other camps. Built out of scaffolding poles, the control tower, near the runway (the landing strip protected all along by sandbags), looks to have been abandoned last, because neither the windows, nor the platform on which the control tower room stands, nor the equipment inside have been damaged. The fugitives look up into the sky. But it's at the end of the runway that they finally notice a silvery steel hulk advancing slowly towards the forest, and then, after stopping at the runway's edge, make a U-turn and, ready for take-off, come to a halt between two strips of grass. Two powerful jet engines, fixed to two very large wings, start thrumming, begin to roar, begin emitting two air streams even more powerful than the wind. The grass and bushes behind are flattened in a split second; the piercing noise the jets emit reaches the fugitives' ears, louder than the howling storm. Immobile, completely impenetrable from the outside, the machine crouching at the end of the plateau dominates the landscape. The cabin windows look blank, the windows in the cockpit reflect only the grey sky; but there must be someone inside, the fugitives are thinking. At this moment, tons of steel driven by jet engines start moving. Stunned, completely powerless to make themselves known to the machine as it gathers speed, the fugitives understand that they are forsaken: forsaken by God (as always), forsaken by men (since the soldiers drove them out of their homes), forsaken by machines which are supposed to help them survive. Only the mute one stretches out her arms and starts running towards the plane hurtling down the runway. But the plane's wings make no answer as she runs through the grass, waving desperately. Twenty seconds into the run, the plane's nose lifts skyward, the wheels leave the ground, and a hundred tons of steel, leaving in its wake a cloud of dust and burned fuel, takes off. The roaring engines, at full thrust as the plane comes out of a long bank, ease off, and the mute one, watching the plane vanish into the clouds, comes to a stop before the empty runway. The fugitives look at the parcels strewn around. Medicine and food must have been air-dropped here. But like land relief operations, air-drops of food supplies are now considered too complex and too risky; war missions such as these (in this hostile environment) give rise to unpredictable results. Either operations are carried out between fifteen and eighteen thousand feet so as to be beyond the range of anti-aircraft batteries (the generals have declared), in which case the pilots cannot ensure that the parcels land where they should; or they are done at low altitude by planes which, of necessity, are slow, and whose crew are then exposed to anti-aircraft fire. The mute one looks at an empty parcel at her feet. In her fury, she kicks it – it lifts off into the sky. 'A kite!' the little girl yells. She too kicks an empty parcel. 'Another kite!' But the mute one points at the forest beyond the airbase runway. 'Is that where the border is?' a woman asks. The man looks at the landscape and the sky. Without the sun, without the morning star, it's difficult to get bearings, and the forest looks the same everywhere, a hostile mass surrounding the windswept plateau. Even the rubbish dump, this shapeless blot behind their backs, offers no possible orientation. Where's north? Where does no man's land begin? From somewhere, a burst of machine-gun fire resounds. The mute one and the man look at each other. The army is still here, ready to fight, ready to pursue those it wishes to exterminate, and there's no shortage of guns, soldiers, ammunition, tanks, military bases, fuel, combat equipment. 'Somewhere down there, there must be a river,' the man says, pointing towards the trees bending in the wind. 'That's where the border is.'

19

'None of you, who are still alive, want to talk?' asks the commander, holding the woman impaled on his member. 'No one?' he asks the prisoners. The man shot in the head with the revolver and the motor oil drinker executed by machine-gun fire will never talk again. The prisoner who tortures (lying in a dead faint between the legs of the woman tied down on the bed) and the castrated one (lying on top of the dead prisoners) don't look too talkative either. 'Four bastards,' says the commander, counting. 'And the fifth one?' His gaze pierces the prisoner whose back is against the wall. 'You're their leader. We should have executed you before anyone else. You're the sort who lets his comrades die when you could be saving them. All you have to do is tell us where your allies are!' The prisoner doesn't answer. The commander pulls his cock out of the woman he's just shafted and, with a movement full of menace, unsheathes the knife strapped to his calf. 'Look at this body,' he says to the prisoner. 'Perfect breasts, flat belly, soft skin, a deliciously slender waist, a juicy cunt. Do you know this woman?' The prisoner doesn't speak. 'Bring him here!' The officers push the prisoner before their chief. 'Of course you know her!' he screams. 'She was – and always has been – your mistress!' He grabs hold of his cock and shoves it up her cunt. 'Do you want me to do an autopsy on her in front of you?' The prisoner remains silent. The commander presses the knife to the woman's throat, pierces the skin, waits for the first drops of blood to appear. 'Where are the men we're looking for?' The prisoner persists in his stubborn silence. With a quick, vigorous movement, the commander slits the woman's throat. As blood spurts from severed arteries, splashing the prisoner's face, the knife blade slices the body open from the neck down to the pubis. 'You still refuse to speak?' The officers push the prisoner towards the woman, force his head down over the slashed-open belly, open his mouth – a volley of spunk spurts out of the commander's cock. 'Swallow!' the officers scream. Once the prisoner has gulped it down, they shove his face into the belly. 'Don't drown him,' the commander mutters. A white-hot poker is shoved up the prisoner's rectum. 'Hang him by the feet!' While the officers carry the body off, the commander places a bucket in front of the one woman left standing. 'Piss!' The bucket full, he puts his hands between her legs and shows her his wet fingers. 'So, we don't dry ourselves?' The officers laugh. 'Well, my lovely, if you want to cooperate with us, wake up the scumbag who shopped your girlfriend!' The woman picks up the bucket, goes to the bed where (sprawled between the skewered woman's legs) the prisoner who has fainted lies, and pours the piss over his face. Once he has come to, the officers drag him over to the prisoner hanging up by the feet. 'Get your own back on the pig who let us torture you for nothing!' His eyes staring, the prisoner mechanically sinks his teeth into the belly, tugs, bites again, succeeds in piercing the skin and tears off a piece of flesh. 'Good!' says the commander. 'And now tell us whether he's really your leader – and you're saved!' The prisoner nods. 'It's him?' The prisoner nods again. The commander sticks his index finger and thumb into the prisoner's mouth and extracts the piece of flesh, loads his revolver and asks him in a sceptical tone of voice: 'Did you really think that by torturing your friends you'd save yourself?' And he shoots him dead. 'Splash the one hanging up,' he orders his officers. 'He's still alive. He could still talk.' The officers, after fetching a jerrycan full of petrol, carry out the order. The commander hacks a dead prisoner's arm off, dips the fingers at the end of the stump into the petrol, strikes a match, brings the flame to the dunked fingers, and points the flaming torch at the one woman left standing. 'You didn't even try to throw the piss in my face, you've got such good manners,' says the commander, his mouth curling into a nasty smile. 'Now go and ask their leader in the same good-mannered way whether he'd rather tell us where their allies are, or be burned alive!'

20

The ground beneath his feet gives way. He pushes the cart once more but, on the verge of physical collapse, stops and chocks the wheel with his foot. Fortunately, there's a steel cap in his shoe to protect his toes while he scrabbles about for a stone to jam under the wheel, the wheel that would take the cart (propelled by the weight of dead bodies) back down to the bottom of the mountain that he has only just managed in fits and starts to climb. He'd ended up having to ditch the tractor, found by chance on his return, when after a few miles it ran out of petrol. The rest of the way, he had to push the cart himself. Determined, however, to bring his father, mother and two brothers back to where he lives, he has without the slightest hesitation become a beast of burden, dragging the cart along a rock-strewn road ploughed up by mortar shells. He leans back against the cart. The wheel is chocked, the cart is halfway up the slope he must climb; on the other side of the mountain, the road leads down to the bridge, the only dangerous place in the area. Breathing in the freezing air, he doesn't look at his father, his mother, his two brothers; to look at those he wants to save from extinction (total extinction: where not a single place in the world marks your burial spot) would be impossible: after being brutally murdered, they were flung into a trench dug in the middle of a field so that winter (which erases all proof of crime) would hide their bodies. This monstrous lack of respect (this wilful refusal to accord the dead their burial rights) is the war's infamous guiding principle: the enemy's hateful face revealed! He trembles in fury each time he thinks of their method (mulled over, programmed, systematic). The people running this war aren't soldiers – to shoot civilians, kill farmhands, slaughter unarmed people is the work of criminals. And by refusing to treat the dead as human beings these criminals have become monsters. He looks away from the road leading to the mountain summit; he looks away from the ruts in the ground where his feet (two dusty things at the end of his legs which he has trouble recognising) are jammed between two stones: inches away is a sheer drop to a dry river bed below, which, when the snows thaw, becomes a powerful torrent, carrying stones and tree trunks, animal carcasses and shattered carts. His gaze wanders over the drop; not a single tree, not a patch of scrub has managed to take root in the rock, which (after a pounding from the spring torrents) the wind breaks up better than the pick of any miner (absent, of course, since the beginning of the war). Then something unusual (a colour unlike the uniform grey of the stones) catches his eye. His gaze searches among the rocks, plunges into excavations, comes to a rest at the foot of a block of granite, and scans the place: the granite block by the river bed hangs over a body lying among the rocks. Even before seeing the mutilated breasts and genitals (from which blood has streamed after a fall), he knows it's a woman. He stops breathing. Flung into the ravine after being tortured, she is obscenely contorted (legs spread, arms thrown out), broken to bits, bruised, frozen, like all the corpses that the assassins, deliberately spreading terror, dump at the side of the road. That the murderers threw this woman (who could have been his sister) to the bottom of the ravine confirms that their hatred (which reaches its climax in the rape and murder of women) knows no limits. An insatiable urge to rape women hangs over this scorched earth (something that neither he nor any man on the victims' side can admit). Looking at this woman lying at the bottom of the ravine (a woman whom in any case he cannot take with him), he sees once more (and admits to himself) how bestial the enemy is. He looks away from the ravine, gulps down the freezing air several times, leans into the cart, and takes to the road again, pushing with all his strength.

21

Today, the problem (appearances notwithstanding) is about finding the living. And to shut their mouths. Sometimes when, towards evening, tiredness comes over me (and twilight affects visibility) I feel I am perched not above a besieged city, but on the top of a skyscraper that rises above the centre of a megalopolis. My work remains the same: to find the living who hide in the midst of the dehumanised human tide that my eye (with thousands of cameras to help) surveys unflinchingly. For in the robotic crowd, living men are still hiding, indistinguishable from zombies. How can one tell, in an era of genetic engineering, who, in the anonymous crowd of standardised beings, is still the authentic one? Before, it was enough to remove the mask to reveal a man's identity. The clothes, the airs an individual affected, hid the true man; his identity came fully to light only when outward appearance was done away with. Suspicion and unveiling: the good old method. Which, at the dawn of the millennium of authentic life's extinction, is useless. Suspect! Unveil!

The inquisitor can tear all he likes at what he supposes is the mask; the rent reveals the counterfeit flesh beneath. Where once the impostor concealed his shame, the being manufactured according to industrial norms feels nothing. What hatred has moved man to modify his metaphysical skills? The notion of camouflaging oneself, of becoming somebody else, of inventing a new identity, to invest oneself *freely* in another future, is disappearing from the range of human possibility. Identity is thinkable only through the terrible awareness that it is lacking. This dizziness (which allows the living to experiment with their humanity) our era seeks to eliminate. To robotise, such was the aim of feudalism, powerfully taken up again in the industrial age. Lobotomise, such was the response of societies whose essential characteristic is 'In God We Trust'. Today we live in a *tragic* age which cannot be characterised by any of these former procedures. Progress and science seem to build the future. But men who feel the dizziness of being know that somewhere in the wall of physical laws there is a black hole, which is the cornerstone of the freedom of life. Science plugs up the hole with laws and modified genes; progress wears itself out in denying the void. And as for myself? At one with my gun, I eliminate this hole by plugging another one in the survivors' skulls, through which (like water from a tap) their freedom escapes as so much splattered brain. To arms! I am more honest! More to the point! As science today leads us into a dehumanised universe, future millennia will need obedient men. No predator shall enter into competition with the state. Yes, perhaps my gun is creating a world in which, finally, there will be no place for me. So what? To track down living men (these bearers of freedom characterised by their wild impulses, their ability to act independently, an imagination that escapes physical laws) is my trade. If in my nightmare I cannot pick out of the crowd in the dehumanised megalopolis the authentic ones, here above this besieged city, the minute I open my eyes I see them in the flesh. Isn't my mission to wipe these evil weeds off the surface of the planet? I load my gun. Ready. Fire.

22

Coming to the edge of a wood, the fugitives stop. Tree tops blasted by the storm sway above their heads in a terrifying dance conducted by gusts of wind. Tired out, emaciated, too weak to resist ever more violent flurries, the fugitives cling to the tree trunks to rest. Some chew on pieces of food found in the abandoned camp. Others, squatting, lean back against the moaning timber. The mute one looks at the man. 'No point in checking out this forest,' he says. 'The river's not far. We'll get some strength back, then move off together.' The mute one nods. 'Look,' yells one of the fugitives, pointing at the other side of the plateau. A column of tanks and army trucks has appeared on the horizon. 'Get down and don't move,' says the man. The vehicles at the head of the military convoy come to a halt. An officer looks out of a tank turret, his binoculars sweep the plateau, the armoured cars belch clouds of smoke, the steel cannons shine: the military convoy moves forward in the fugitives' direction. 'They've seen us,' someone cries. 'Impossible,' the man replies. 'They couldn't have seen us.

Anyway, we're way ahead of them, and tanks and armoured cars can't follow us into this jungle.' Behind the mountains, a dozen assault helicopters appear. Flying between two peaks, they head for the plateau. 'They're going to drop commandos,' a woman says, frightened. The mute one stands up from behind a hedge, raises her hand. 'She'll go first,' says the man, 'while you all follow. I'll bring up the rear. And be careful where you step: there could be mines!' While the sound of helicopters gets louder, the fugitives run through the forest. Stones, burrs, fern, the muddy ground, broken branches and mulberry offshoots make it difficult to walk. Helicopters sound above their heads. 'An air patrol,' the man groans. 'But don't worry, the forest is thick, they won't see us.' The helicopters fly over the place where the fugitives are hidden, move away, turn around and head back to the plateau. The mute one keeps moving through the trees, avoiding the undergrowth where it is too thick, stones that are too large, the ground where it is too marshy, then stops as the land falls steeply away. The man catches up with her, looks down the ravine where, one piled on top of the other, wrecks of tractors and buses rust on the slope. 'Another dump,' says the man. 'How did they manage to get them here?' The fugitives try to find a way through this wall of metal. A man stops in front of a twisted heap of steel, no doubt a trailer hit by a missile. 'Their cutting-edge technology,' he yells all of a sudden. 'Shit! Shit! If they want to take us, they'll have to come on foot!' No one reacts to the angry man's rants. The mute one skirts around a heap of charred frames and bodywork, pushes past two piles of steel. A sheet of compressed metal halts her progress. She tries to clamber over it, quickly gives up, walks by the metal wall to the back of a bus that forms part of the barrier. The back window is still intact. The mute one wipes it with some leaves, looks inside, makes a sign for the man to break it. 'Can we get through?' The man looks for a stone or something heavy, finds a metal bar, tells the other fugitives to stand back, and hurls himself at the back window with the bar. The glass cracks, then shatters, then flies off in pieces. Sharp pieces of glass sticking out of the frame are removed; a hole has opened up in the wall. 'I'll go,' the man says. He climbs up on to the frame, looks inside, slips through; now sure that the bus shell is solidly wedged in the wall of metal, he moves forward. The corridor of crushed iron leads to a great gash at the front of the bus where a mortar struck. 'Be careful,' he says. The young girl goes through the bus like a shot. The others follow. The mute one, who has gone last, finds several fugitives sitting in the bus, indifferent to what is going on around them. 'Go without us,' a woman mutters. 'We're done for.' The mute one points the way out of the bus, grimaces, gesticulates. A roaring of planes (followed by anti-aircraft fire) gets louder, fades away. The woman bursts out laughing. 'They're bombing the refineries. No one will drop their bombs here.' The man, furious, hits the bus with his iron bar. 'Come out of there, you won't survive!' The seated fugitives stand up. Those waiting for them outside sift through a heap of tin cans, find helmets and bullet-proof jackets. 'Everyone ready?' the man asks. The mute woman leads the group. Wearing helmets and bullet-proof jackets, the fugitives slide down through the muck, their skinny torsos protected as though they were a paramilitary commando. Another formation of fighter jets flies over the forest. The fugitives look up at the sky, see only the tree tops, blasted by the wind and the jet motors' echoes. The mute one stops. The pass through which they must go is blocked by a vast mound of corpses. 'Instead of digging mass graves, they dumped them here,' says the man. The mute one looks at the fugitives. They will never be able to climb back up the slope, too steep even for an equipped mountaineer. In any case, most of them don't even seem to realise what could be holding them back. As for those who are still lucid, they stare fixedly at the ground. The man climbs over the bodies. At the top of the mound, he looks towards the bottom of the ravine. 'We can get down,' he says. The mute one urges the fugitives on. 'Follow me,' the man yells. 'You'll see that the slope gets less steep, and the river isn't far!' The first fugitive climbs up. Then another. 'Bodies are resistant as long as they're alive,' the man mutters. 'Dead, they won't last a season!' Clutching at tree roots, grabbing at dead people's arms, leaning against rocks, sticking their fingers into the muddy earth, the fugitives descend. Their feet slipping on frozen corpses, their fingers grazing against skin swollen up in the cold, they slide and fall, whimper, then, having got down, backs bowed and speechless, they walk between craters thrown up by mortar shells. At the bottom of the slope, river water reflects through the trees.

23

A grenade detonates, blows open the door of head office at HQ. Before the officers can do anything, the blonde woman, standing at the threshold, sprays them with assault-rifle fire. 'Fuckers!' The commander throws himself to the ground, yelling orders, brandishes his revolver, shoots several times, misses his target, holds his gun with both hands to aim better. The other woman, the one left standing, holds up the burning arm and sticks this torch made of flesh into his mouth. The commander manages to shoot again, tries to get the stump out of his mouth. The other officers fire at the woman holding the assault rifle, who, trying to see which of the women is still alive, protects herself behind the body of a dead officer (who she holds by the neck like a shield). Bullets tear into the officer's body without hurting the woman. Another officer, hidden behind the metal bed, loads his rifle. The woman hears the magazine click, aims her assault rifle in his direction, waits until he raises his head, and fires a volley of bullets at his throat. The officer slumps to the floor, dropping his loaded weapon. Now that the shooting has stopped, the girl next to the commander wants to seize the initiative and get the rifle; but there's life in the commander yet. She smashes the arm holding the gun, with a metal bar shatters his wrist so that he drops the revolver, picks it up, shoots a bullet into his skull, and fires another at an officer hiding behind the desk. The officer, protected by the desk (where the disembowelled woman still lies), returns fire several times. Wounded in the arm, the girl with the revolver runs over to the girl pinned down by dead prisoners, drags her out from under these inert corpses, points out the rifle on the floor, gives her cover by shooting at the officer behind the desk. The freed woman gets hold of the rifle and shoots the last surviving officer. 'Out of here!' says the blonde woman. The woman holding the revolver cuts down the prisoner hanging by the feet and, having realised that he has no chance of surviving his wounds, shoots him in the head. 'Let's go!' Armed with assault rifles, the three women cross the corridor. The stairway is empty. 'Two floors to go!' Out of a door on the left comes a soldier, his uniform dishevelled. His inebriated gaze falls on the women. 'Hang on, I was just about to fetch one of you!' He opens the bedroom door again, points at one of the girls. 'I quite fancy you!' But instead of going into the soldier's room, the woman takes him by the arm, shoves his shocked body into the corridor, closes the door, and sinks a knife into his chest. While the soldier's blood spreads across the floor tiles, the women go down the stairs. The sound of an engine tells them that a military vehicle is pulling into the yard. 'Let's take their motor!' says one of the women, seeing an officer's jeep through a spyhole in the security door that gives on to the courtyard. 'Wait till they go away,' says the blonde. They take a breather, backs against the security door's steel surface. 'So are they away yet?' 'They're going to the bar, let's wait a bit more!' In the building's silent corridors, a door creaks, alerting them to the presence of other soldiers. 'Let them come nearer,' says the blonde. 'We'll fire at point-blank range only!' The women hide the guns behind their backs, smooth their dresses, push out their breasts. Two soldiers appear at the bottom of the stairs leading to the basement. Uniforms unbuttoned, machine guns hanging from their shoulders, they chat as they go up the steps. 'Fucking hell, I've never shagged so much in my life! Signing up was well worth it!' 'A dozen birds a day...Who would have thought it!' 'You're right...Hold on, there's three more.' 'But there's only two of us...' 'Not to worry, we'll bump one off straight away!' One of the soldiers points his machine gun at the women leaning against the security door. 'Which one shall I waste?' 'They've all got big tits, better have a closer look!' The girls smile. 'Come here, you can fuck us one after the other! With your big cocks, that shouldn't be a problem!' The soldier holding the machine gun staggers in the stairway. 'Which one of them thinks she can give us advice?' 'The one in the middle. Shoot her!' 'OK...

you're right, there's something dodgy about her!' The soldier pushes a magazine into his weapon. But just at the moment when it is lowered, no longer aimed at the women, he and the other soldier die in a hail of bullets. 'Is the yard empty now?' 'Yes, let's go!' 'Who'll drive?' 'I will. You shoot the sentries!'

24

He stops the cart. The road heads straight towards the stone bridge (which enemy aircraft bombed in the meantime, damaging several supporting pillars; but the bridge still stands, the cart will pass). Potholes, bumps and branches fallen on to the road make the corpses in the cart jump as the wheels turn; they move, collide, elbow and jostle each other as though fighting for the right to a place in this cart which will take them to their graves over the scorched mountain. Arms and legs stiff, eyes sparkling, their expressions as indignant as ever, they seem at the same time to be mocking the efforts their son and brother is making; above all the father, his arm raised to heaven, his jaw wide open, looks as though he is laughing at what is happening, and cursing what has come to pass: disgusted by the cowardice of the murderers he never stops seeing before him, he persists (with stubbornness and wrath) in standing up to those he considers hateful and vile, to deny the existence of these loathsome bastards of the human race, these perpetrators of the most despicable injustice. Still amazed by this inconceivable eruption of the bestial into the lives of ordinary people, the raging old man fights back, as he fought back in death, in the excruciating knowledge that it was useless to fight back (old and unarmed before soldiers with machine guns), raising his arm to fend off the bullets fired at him, yelling curses at those who had already killed his wife and two sons. His wife, still behind him (even as he struggled against the criminals' overwhelming force), her face full of bitter surprise (why this extermination?), full of eternal regret (they have murdered my sons!), full of unshakeable defiance (you will not shoot!) and an absolute refusal to forgive this barbarity: since her youth (marked by the war), she had lived her whole life in the hope that neither war nor crime would ever again ravage her country. The slaughter of animals (pigs, cows, chickens) was the only killing her peasant's soul allowed. But her country became a slaughterhouse again. In many ways, she had lived long enough – but to die in such a way: killed by bloodthirsty madmen, killed like an animal not even worth the price of one! It is the murder of her two sons, however, unacceptable murder, gratuitous carnage, which most distressed her: never again should anyone be allowed to commit acts like these! Her two sons, riddled with bullets a few seconds later, lie before their father, mown down for having run at the soldiers with nothing in their hands (nothing but the stone the youngest held in his fist): automatics were already levelled at them, the criminals' fingers had already squeezed the triggers, but not for a single instant did the brothers waver as they ran at their despicable murderers, rejecting this horrible massacre (even more horrible because completely arbitrary, conceived in hateful brains, provoked by a sickening will to conquer): they defied this inhuman contempt for human life, fighting the hatred that blinded these swine armed to the teeth, pathetic murderers who didn't give a second's thought to killing old people and children. He brakes the cart, leaning into the front rail. And while he tries to slow it down, as it gathers speed on the hill, the corpses, shaken by several powerful jolts, rise up behind him and scream, cry, insult, rage as though, any more resistance being absolutely futile (are they not all dead, after all?), they resist in spite of everything (with screams, laughter, cries, imprecations) because all they had time for (in the situation that was theirs: of facing death) was the chance to defy their killers!

25

I load my gun. My greatness, my unprecedented role in the history of mankind, I owe to this piece of steel: the moment man can kill at a distance (without taking any personal risk), space (and universal logic with it) is knocked out of kilter. Every bullet I fire concludes that lengthy chapter in world history, that era when men took responsibility for what they did because they did it with their bare hands. If they killed, they killed what was within their reach (and in killing were spattered with the victim's blood: to put it another way, when you kill with your own two hands, you do so in full knowledge of the facts, otherwise the sense of guilt – which keeps at bay the bestial urge in every man – will well up in you). In recent times, we've been killing from a distance. Like magic. A man lying in wait at the top of a mountain (or sitting in front of a computer screen) can consign thousands to oblivion with a single movement of his finger. And his hands are clean! Where is remorse? Where can guilt take hold? If a killer's hands are no longer drenched in blood, then there are no limits to crime. Magical weapons give rise to a new order. You think I belong to the last century? Not at all. I step lightly from one century to the next. A new millennium welcomes me. My weapon – this technological instrument – makes me timeless. When I hold it tight to me, I am no longer a human body: I am a gun. A piece of steel, perfect to behold. A metallic instrument, a machine manufactured according to the latest technological advances. Cruelty requires precision. I am the supremely armed right hand of the force that controls the world. Systematically. Unfailingly. For centuries, man sustained his spiritual needs through prayer and chants. Today he accedes to the celestial spheres by being one with his machine. Mine is a gun. A technological monster capable of overseeing the age, of compressing space, concentrating time into a single point – and blowing it all up in a split second! Men are prisoners of a physical world? I live in another dimension. Create the future. Hate living men. And the limits their anatomical structure imposes. Others carry out the same work in prison camps, research institutes, laboratories, slaughterhouses. They accuse me of killing children? Their flesh incarnates the coming age. Whistling bullets and crashing bombs proclaim a justice better suited to this future world, a justice that the sniper above the ruins of the cleansed city celebrates. Dying of thirst in your rat-infested cellars? Tormented by hunger in basements full of muck? Come out of there! Your troubles will soon be over (in the time it takes to load the rifle, aim, pull the trigger)! At the dawn of this new age, my bullets shall convey those beings who stubbornly cling to the old ways (living men) to the tomb of eternity. The world has changed. The weapons used to uphold order too. Find your prey, point your gun, take aim, fire: the orders that lay the groundwork for the millennia to come are clear! I act according to a plan. No one can fool an elite sniper. Shoot anything (at a human level) that moves. Strength lies in accuracy. Speed. Oh, joy! May glory reward the army of the strong. Rise up, reactionaries of all persuasions! The world rotates on a new axis. The axis of the millennia to come. Where I the sniper will leap for joy.

26

The fugitives stop before the river. Overflowing, bursting its banks, it carries tree trunks, animal carcasses, ice floes, clothes. In a downriver inlet, the current has washed up the mangled remains of dead men. Women, mutilated before being killed, lie on the stony shore. The fugitives look at the water. 'How are we going to get across?' asks the man who screamed with rage in the forest. The mute one points upriver. 'We'll be able to ford it somewhere up there,' says the man beside her. 'Isn't there a bridge?' a woman groans. 'We're at the border,' says the man. 'We've got to get to the other side without a patrol seeing us.' Discouraged, having more and more trouble getting their breath back, the fugitives sigh wearily. 'Everybody stick together,' says the man. 'And keep your eyes open. There are speedboat patrols, they come out of nowhere fast.' 'That's about all I can take,' yells the enraged man. 'Trudge through this muck? Find a ford? Enough's enough!' He picks up a branch, runs along the river's edge, jumps on to the first ice floe big enough to carry him. 'Wait for me!' shouts a woman, running after him. 'Wait for me!' The man slips on the ice as the current bears him along, paddles with the branch, falls into the water, manages to grab hold of a piece of floating timber, screams as another ice floe crushes his fingers, vanishes beneath the waves. 'Wait,' cries the woman running along the river bank. All of a sudden she looks at the ground and notices in the grass a pile of recently turned-over earth, thinks of a molehill, sees a piece of metal, instinctively throws out her hands and tries to sidestep it; but no sooner does she plant her foot a few inches away from the molehill than the mine explodes and kills her instantly. 'I told you to stick together,' yells the man. 'There are mines everywhere, the entire border zone is mined!' Once the fugitives have calmed down, the man picks up a long branch, fashions it into a staff, walks along the river bank poking at the ground before him. The mute one stays at the back of the group. At the first bend in the river, the man stops. A small island cuts the river in two; a good place to cross. The man turns to the mute one. 'Shall we try to cross here?' The mute one nods. 'Night's falling, we won't get much farther anyway,' the man adds. The fugitives agree. Better to jump in the water, go for broke, than stagger along the muddy river bank. The man raises his staff to poke at the ground before him. The minute it touches the ground, there is an explosion, then a spray of earth. Covered in mud and tufts of grass, the man is still standing; he doesn't move, doesn't scream. Clumps of earth drop around the mine crater as the fugitives look at the man's hand. Intact, it convulsively grips the broken staff.

The mute one runs to the man, stops beside him without touching him. After a moment's silence the man opens his eyes. 'Alive,' he says. The mute one takes his paralysed hands and kneads them. 'I'll be all right,' he says. 'Let's go.' The mute one fashions a new staff. The man takes it, makes towards a point opposite the island around which the water looks shallow enough for the fugitives to attempt a crossing. The fugitives hear the sound of bombing carried along on the wind, confirming that the paramilitary units behind them, far from having been wiped out in air attacks, continue (until the next round of attacks begin) to mop up the region. The fugitives stop opposite the island. The mute one stands beside the man. They look at the waves. The water surges between rocks, the main current carries a dangerous load of ice and tree trunks. 'We've got to try,' says the man. The mute one points to the river's edge. 'We'll go down here,' the man tells the fugitives. 'And careful with the current, help each other out when the going gets difficult.' The sound of an outboard engine resounds in the river valley. The fugitives look at the island, then at the bushes at the edge of the wood they have just left. A hundred yards lie between them and a hiding place. 'Everyone into the water,' the man yells. 'The field's mined. We've got to hide on the island.' The fugitives make for the river's edge, a mine goes off under a man's foot, the shock wave throws the young girl into the water, the mute one hurries across the rapids to rescue her daughter before the current takes her away. 'Grab hold of the rocks, take each other by the hand!' the man cries. The fugitives fight against the river, hold on to rocks, avoid blocks of ice carried along by the current. At the most turbulent part of the river, the man wounded in the mine explosion and the woman helping him are swept away. As the first fugitives reach the island, the sound of the outboard engine gets louder. 'Get down,' the man shouts. 'Get down so they won't see you.' The fugitives throw themselves to the ground, crawl through the reeds, seeking to reach the clump of bushes past the marshland they are now vanishing into. From round the bend, the military patrol boat gives chase to the wounded man and the woman, swimming in the middle of the river. The soldiers load their rifles as the boat pulls alongside them, then gunshots ring out. The man looks through the reeds to see what has happened. The patrol – guns at the ready – is heading back towards the island. 'Keep down, they're coming!' The motor rumbles, the boat pulls up to the shore. 'Don't move, they'll stay in the boat!' the man whispers. The soldiers look at the island, shoot at random into the shrubs and bushes. 'We really fucked those two up, didn't we?' says one. 'Do you think there are any more?' 'You never know,' says the officer. 'Let's see if we can flush them out!' The soldier pulls the pin out of a grenade, tosses it on to the island. 'If there's anyone there, we've sent them to heaven.' A flash of light, followed by a series of landmine explosions, throws up a giant mound of earth. The soldiers fire their automatics again, then the boat goes around the island. 'I don't think there's anyone,' says one. 'Any of you want to go and check this shithole out?' asks the officer. 'If I was sure I'd find a bit of skirt…' says the second soldier.

'You could go back and poke the one you just wasted.' 'She was too ugly.' 'Why don't we go back to the mill and see what's left? Back at HQ they'll have heard us firing shots. And there's nothing to say there aren't any others hiding there.' The soldier reloads his gun. 'You're right, we'd better give it one more look over.' The on-board radio crackles. The officer bends towards the microphone. 'Two soft targets eliminated. Surveillance mission continues. Next objective, the mill.' The soldiers laugh. 'Nice one, chief!' The outboard engine thrums, the prow rises, the boat pulls away. On the island, nothing moves. A drizzle falls on the trees and bushes, fog shrouds the craters the explosions have thrown up. As night falls, an insubstantial shadow, followed by other shadows, appears in the fading light. Motionless at first, the shadows then crawl through the reeds and bushes towards the other side of the island, then slip into the river water.

27

Woken by the sound of shooting, a soldier jumps out of bed. Another burst of gunfire rings out in the HQ front yard. 'What's going on?' The soldier opens his bedroom door, steps out into the corridor, sees two soldiers dead in the stairway. 'What the fuck...' The half-open door to head office catches his attention. He thinks for a minute, goes back to his room, grabs his machine gun and makes for the office. Another soldier lies on the ground in a pool of blood, stabbed in the chest. 'Shit!' The soldier loads his magazine, kicks the door wide open, bursts in, yelling: 'Hands up!' Utter silence greets his words. He sees the commander's bullet-riddled corpse, the officers' mangled remains, splayed women, dead prisoners. 'Fucking hell!' Stunned by the sight of his massacred comrades, he doesn't know what to do. Looking back at the soldiers lying in the corridor, he remembers the shots he heard in the front yard. 'Bastards!' He backs out of the office, goes down the stairs, runs to the main entrance. The first thing he sees is the smashed road barrier. Then he sees the windows in the sentry box, shattered by bullets. 'Shit!' He swings around, machine gun at the ready. But the front yard is deserted. Hesitating for a moment, he rushes towards the sentry box, opens the door, steps over a pool of blood, heaves the dead sentries aside, dials a number. 'Hello?' Having put the phone down, he gazes in amazement at the roadblock with its unending line of refugees. Buses, carts, cars, tractors and trailers move slowly between pyramidal stacks of sandbags laid down in an S formation so as to regulate the flow. The border is some way off, but leaving their homes has given the expelled villagers hope. If they manage to get out of the area under the army's control, then it doesn't matter how many days it will take to get to the border crossing. Soldiers check vehicles, demand to see papers if they don't like the look of a refugee, demand money, call those too poor to pay dirty bastards as they send them off. 'What a pain,' an officer whines. 'The rich have already left, and the poor break our balls!' 'The rich are always first to go,' says a soldier. 'But don't believe it, there's always something you can swipe.' From around a bend in the road, a jeep goes past a halted bus, overtakes the line of refugees. The driver sounds the horn at trailers blocking the way, swings past smashed-up vehicles, hitting the horn again with a vengeance as the jeep comes up to the roadblock. The soldiers, seeing an officers' jeep, clear a passage through the refugee traffic. 'Let it through.' The jeep pulls up beside the bus stopped at the control. The officer, who knows this jeep, goes to the driver's window. Unusually, the window doesn't come down. 'What are you hiding?' The officer laughs. The jeep pushes on past him. 'Playing hard to get? Listen, everyone obeys my orders here. What are you hiding?' The soldier, coming back out of the stopped bus, starts complaining: 'Real down-and-outs, these ones. They've got nothing. Not even girls.' He sees the jeep. 'Shit, there's...' he says, surprised to see a blonde girl inside. 'Three, even,' he adds, peering in. 'What?' the officer asks. 'So that's why they don't want me to see what they've got.' Someone gets out of an army truck parked by the roadblock. 'Commander, there's been an attack at HQ. It seems that...' Filled with foreboding all of a sudden, the officer approaches the jeep, hand on his gun holster, but the window has already been rolled down, and a rifle sticking out of it fires. The officer falls. 'Bitches,' the soldier yells, loading his magazine. Another burst of gunfire rings out, killing him, then the soldier who has just got out of the truck parked near the roadblock. As two automatic rifles gun down more soldiers running towards the roadblock, the jeep crashes through the sandbags, overtakes the bus full of refugees, crushes several soldiers and petrol canisters, smashes through the barrier that blocks the road, and heads off into the distance as army trucks explode, spraying the arms depot with petrol. 'It's OK, we're through!' yells one of the girls. At full speed, the jeep heads for the border.

28

The cartwheels creak; he leans against the rail. At the end of the street stands his house (still in the same state: the roof caved in by bombs, the walls pockmarked with bullets, collapsed wooden beams blocking the front entrance, the garden torched). He has only a hundred yards to go; now it seems almost certain that he will bring his father's, mother's and brothers' bodies home. Thus he will have saved them from that disappearance their murderers had intended: he will dig them a grave in the city cemetery, lay their bodies in a place where winter cannot efface their death. After many miles on the road, he can finally look at them: they are there, in the cart, his father with his arm raised to the heavens, his eyes wide open, his mother still behind him, full of bitter regret, and his two brothers (the youngest holding a stone). The struggle undertaken to bring them all this way exhausts him more now than during the journey. He sees again the field in which they were buried, he smells the earth he struck at, he remembers the axe he left at the bottom of the hole, after freeing the dead from the frozen ground; he hears the last gasp of the tractor that broke down in the middle of the devastated countryside, he sees once more the woman, arms and legs splayed, lying at the bottom of the ravine. His hands are covered with a mixture of mud and the blood that flowed from his flesh, split by the axe handle and the cart shaft. But he doesn't think of this; he looks at the corpses in the cart, these frozen bodies which, in the winter cold, herald the beginning of the end for the killers' triumph: nothing will conceal (ever again) their crimes! Like him, other men will go looking for the dead beneath the iced-over earth, where the killers (aided by the jaws of bulldozers) imprisoned them: all the mass graves dug in the fields (into which army trucks tipped dozens of the dead, like rotting animal carcasses, all the mine shafts (where, in a systematic attempt to cover up all traces of murder – a plan conceived by minds obsessed with safeguarding their impunity – hundreds of anonymous people were held captive), all the country's wells and underground galleries (into which countless victims disappeared), men like him will search to reveal their secrets. He breathes the icy air. The dead, which the killers (in spite of speeches larded with proclamations as to how they had the right to act as they did) wished to hide so as to conceal their crimes, are here all of a sudden: they come running from all sides, arms raised to the heavens, eyes wide open, mouths screaming their rejection of murder, torture, rape and massacre; these dead are led by the old man who, with his exploded chest, his staring eyes, his mouth wide open, was first to rise out of the earth, lifting his arm, leading the rebellion of the dead against death, against ignorance of death and against the most despicable will in the world, the will to conceal murder perpetrated in the criminal blindness of injustice without bounds!

29

A cart? Pushed by a halfwit? This man coming back from the mountain with a pile of corpses must be mentally deficient. An abnormal and dangerous man, therefore. I killed the messenger. I'll kill this nutter just as quickly. Exhausted, haggard, he stops at a crossroad of devastated streets. His wife, several months pregnant, stands in front of their ruined home. She is waving at him. Crying. Sobbing. If it hadn't been for her husband's homecoming, the sow would never have come out of her hole. With her belly. Fat like a drum. She looks around her, gazes at the bushes and hills, where the snow, since the bombs, has turned into a horrifying mire of blood, corpses, rotting flesh, shrapnel, an awful mush oozing down the charred mountain side. She is afraid (my child must live, she thinks). But she feels compelled, in spite of such cares, to run into her hero's arms, because the emotions reunions inspire are all too overwhelming. The man, this headcase who has risked his life to dig up his family's bodies, yells at her to hide. 'There's a sniper!' I aim. Where shall I hit her? If I go for the head, the little fucker might live. Better if I get her in the belly. Slap bang in the paunch (where babykins already stirs). Patience. In a few seconds, she'll run to her darling husband. Who I will execute before her very eyes (before she can hold him). But I must stay calm. She is my real prey. A pregnant woman. Symbol of life. A murdered husband means only one more dead body. Nothing the survivors would find impressive. A different order of slaughter is needed. To sacrifice that which has never been sacrificed. A guttersnipe crushed as it is born, a pregnant woman killed, that's what we need. Horror in its purest form! The ultimate sacrifice! To descend into the depths of crime even to the umbilical cord, to extinguish a possible birth, there's my duty. I load my gun. What? I've only two bullets left. Amazement! Anxiety! I look at the mountain. Charred earth, empty roads, carbonised rubble, silent valleys: nothing suggesting that ammunition is on its way. What negligence! What shirking of responsibility! The army is not allowed to miss delivery dates. Such dysfunction terrifies me. To prevent a sniper from shooting at such a crucial moment is a crime against order. What do my superiors want? That I croak? Bullets – I have only two (I'm forced to confirm, having counted again). One for the woman, one for the man. And for me? What if, for some reason (mounting cold, lack of food, ambush by scouts, sudden enemy advance), I wanted to do away with myself! Horror (I don't give a fuck about a brat, his head splattered the moment he comes out of his mother's womb) is to live defenceless at the heart of the disaster. Dead towns, smashed bridges, calcinated mountains, thousands of rotting corpses – that sort of horror you get used to. You even start asking for more (especially when you've caused it at zero personal risk). But to be condemned to wait for your own death (alone and unarmed, a victim of fate) is terror. And terror (this intimate knowledge of what has caused the disaster) plunges man into a suffocating universe, where victims' hands point and gesticulate, accusing those who helped women give birth by firing bullets dead centre into their bellies, condemning those who (having sunk to the depths of depravity) lord it in the ruins. It's here, in a universe of annihilation and cruelty, that ethics grab hold of man. Can humanity survive as it sinks into crimes as heinous as murdered births? All I know (I who care nothing for guilt, who despise moral preachers, who am a block of marble armed and enthroned on a block of steel at the concrete entrance to an underground gallery, who am THE MONSTER OF INHUMANITY (seized now with fear owing to lack of ammunition) is that mankind has entered the era of self-destruction!